Bonita Palms

A NOVEL

Hal Ross

Bonita Palms

© Hal Ross. ALL RIGHTS RESERVED.

Authored by Hal Ross

       Published by TitleTown Publishing
       Green Bay, Wisconsin
       www.titletownpublishing.com

No part of this book may be reproduced in any form or by any means, electronic or mechanical, including photocopying, recording, taping, or by any storage and retrieval system, without the written permission of Hal Ross or TitleTown Publishing.

Interior design © TitleTown Publising
Cover design © TitleTown Publising
Cover photos © TitleTown Publishing. ALL RIGHTS RESERVED

ISBN (hardcover): 978-1-949042-16-0
This title is also available in electronic and audiobook formats.

PUBLISHER'S CATALOGING-IN-PUBLICATION DATA
Ross, Hal
BONITA PALMS / ROSS
1st edition. Green Bay, WI: TitleTown Publishing, c2019.

                  Proudly Printed in the United States of America
                             10 9 8 7 6 5 4 3 2 1

Pour Francine, pour toujours

ACKNOWLEDGMENTS

This book would not have been possible without the help of Cliff Carle, an extraordinary editor.

A few paragraphs on the development of prescription medication are paraphrased from an unpublished novel by Dr. Ron Porter.

The author used poetic license in the physical descriptions and various situations in which we find the fictional mayors of Ft. Myers and Bonita Springs, Florida, and no correlation shown be drawn between them and the actual mayors of both cities, for whom the author has great respect.

PROLOGUE

January 4

The doorbell ringing surprised her...

She glanced at her watch, a gold Rolex with a diamond bezel. Her first thought was that it must be the pizza. But barely fifteen minutes had passed since she'd placed her order. She set her wine glass down on the coffee table, stood and went to see who it was.

"H...Hello," came the awkward greeting.

"Oh, hi," she said, smiling.

"Sorry to bother you."

"No bother at all." She opened the door wider.

"I—uh—need to borrow a pipe wrench. Do you happen to have one?"

"Yes, I do."

"Great. Damn leak under our kitchen sink is getting worse."

"No problem. Just give me a minute."

"I'll wait here," her visitor said, stepping into the foyer and closing the door.

Her destination was the workshop inside the garage. She flipped on the light switch. Her gaze automatically traversed the power drill, floor model electric saw, lathe, and various other objects that befit a do-it-yourselfer; something her husband was not but pretended to be.

It didn't take long to locate the wrench, hanging on a hook. She shut off the light, cradled the implement in her arm, and carried it back to her visitor.

"Here you go," she said, passing it off, and turned, meaning to reopen the front door.

The first strike, aimed for the head, missed and caught the back of her shoulder, but with enough force to drop her to her knees.

The pain was excruciating. *My God, what just happened?* she wondered.

She twisted and looked up, scarcely in time to see the wrench coming at her again. Instinctively, she tried to block it.

The second strike broke her arm; she screamed.

There was a strange look in her assailant's eyes. Confusion? Regret? And this gave her hope.

She was struggling to get to her feet when the third strike opened a gash close to her carotid artery on the left side of her neck.

Why? she wanted to ask.

Too late, the fourth strike pulverized her skull.

1

Six hours earlier

Cathy Sinclair liked her life, and very much enjoyed living in Bonita Palms. The Gulf Coast community in Bonita Springs, Florida, had been her second home for the past eleven years. Originally from St. Louis, Missouri, Cathy and her husband, Frank, still maintained a condo in the city of their birth, but rarely spent time there.

A gated community, "The Palms" as most residents referred to it, boasted a challenging golf course, three tennis courts, a fitness club, an Olympic-sized swimming pool, multiple bicycle and walking trails, and two separate and impressive dining facilities. Over two thousand acres in all. A heartbeat west of US 41, the Palms bragged that they were close enough to Naples without coming across as ostentatious, and far enough from Fort Myers without being lumped in with what some considered, perhaps snobbishly so, a semi-blue-collar town.

What Cathy liked most about where she lived was the proximity to restaurants and shops that were dear to her heart. Even better, when it came to the weather, she believed few other locations in North America could compare. It was as if there were an invisible demarcation line sixty miles south of Sarasota, protecting this part of Florida from not only excessive rain but the cold.

Twenty-one hundred homes and condominiums in all, with values varying from four hundred thousand to fifteen million dollars. The Palms was self-sufficient, owned and managed by the members themselves. The current board of directors had Cathy convinced that the worst was over. They'd come through recessionary times. They'd survived the downturn in golf's popularity. They'd outlasted a major mortgage crisis.

As she strolled through her fifty-two hundred square-foot house, Cathy was reminded that the cathedral ceiling contributed to a feeling of unrestricted space. She entered the huge bathroom adjoining the master bedroom and took a seat on the upholstered bench in front of the full-length mirror.

She slipped out of her rose-colored nightgown and a self-satisfied smile creased her lips. Sixty-two years old and the breasts of a woman half her age, with only the slightest imperfection— the left being slightly larger than the right. Though her doctor told her it was normal; nature's way of adding extra protection for her heart.

She turned, first to one side, then the other. At five-five, she was proud of her well-distributed weight of 116 pounds. Her blonde hair may have its share of peroxide, her Botox treatments may have contributed to the appealing shape of her lips and cheeks, but Cathy took pride in her appearance. Unlike some, she never denied the fact that she'd had various enhancements. Plus, she was pleased with the results, and that was all that mattered.

She glanced at the wall clock adjacent to the mirror and

chided herself. She stood, slipped into her bra and panties, then approached her closet—nearly the length and width of an average-sized bedroom—to pick out what she planned to wear.

Early January yet the temperature had been unseasonably warm. She was tempted to choose the white cardigan, but was mindful of the time of year. Summer colors could wait for summer, she decided, finally selecting a navy blue, two-piece pants suit that she believed to be more appropriate.

In the kitchen she donned oven mitts, lifted the meatloaf casserole from the top of the stove where she'd left it to cool, inserted it into a thermal wrap, then headed to the garage.

* * *

Fifteen minutes later, she steered her E-450 Mercedes into the parking lot of the Anglican Church on Bonita Beach Boulevard.

Her five neighbors, who were also her best friends, were already in the kitchen. Air kisses made the rounds. First with Jill Derbyshire, a thin redhead, well-put-together sixty-seven-year-old from Cleveland, Ohio. Jill was wearing tan slacks and a cardigan in white; the very color Cathy had told herself to avoid.

Denise Gerigk, a Montreal-born French-Canadian blonde, now living primarily in Toronto, at fifty-eight, wasn't merely the second youngest of the group but the best looking; not surprisingly making her the most envied. Denise was attired in a burgundy, form-fitting dress that accented her curves in a distinctive way.

Cynthia Gladstone, a sixty-three-year-old originally from Detroit, was another attractive blonde, of average height, wearing a light blue, Coral Bay golf dress that was not out of place away from the golf course.

Debbie Stafford stood next to her, a brunette in her mid-sixties from Louisville, Kentucky; a heavy-set woman attired in what could only be described as a coral-colored muumuu.

And finally, Barbara Miller, a tall, statuesque woman, in black head to toe: sweater, skirt, and shoes. Barbara, also a brunette, was a forty-nine-year-old from Buffalo, New York. The other women aptly described her as a trophy wife.

"Meals for Humanity" was their charity of choice. Twice a week they took turns preparing appetizer, salad, main course, dessert, and beverage—usually coffee—and bringing it here, where they volunteered their time to serve the homeless.

Cathy found it a blessing and not a chore.

Today, there were over fifty people. Mexicans, African Americans, and whites. The downtrodden; men and a few women. Most had seen better times; some had never seen good times at all.

There, but for the grace of God... flittered through Cathy's head uninvited. She well knew what it was like to be poor. And while she and members of her immediate family had never hit the same depths as some of these people, she felt sorry for them. Though this was an emotion she would never display, knowing how fickle their pride was.

The first in line was a man Cathy knew simply as Joe. He was well past sixty-five. A weather-beaten face, unkempt gray hair worn far too long. His fingernails varied in size and were discolored. Cathy filled his plate and bid him a pleasant day.

A man Cathy hadn't seen before followed. Then a woman who broke Cathy's heart. Cindy Travis was barely thirty, yet looked far older. Today the bruises on her face were more pronounced. The diminutive woman was a bundle of nerves, trembling as she proffered her plate with an anxious hand.

"Cindy…" Cathy kept her voice as low as possible so as not to embarrass her. "Can we talk afterwards? I … want to help. If you won't go to the women's shelter I suggested, let me come up with another solution."

The woman's eyes enlarged. "Shh–" she hissed, then mumbled something else.

Cathy couldn't make out what she said; it sounded like "He's here." Or, "He's near." She looked around. She'd met Cindy's husband once before, a disgruntled laggard with a chip on his shoulder. A man twice the size of his wife and prone to violence.

Before Cathy could say anything more, Cindy hurried away. Cathy reluctantly went back to her chore. The line was long. It took over twenty-five minutes before the last could be served.

* * *

The six ladies regrouped in the kitchen. The large portrait of Christ on the near wall overpowered the room. And while it should have acted as a monitor of decorum, it had little effect on Cathy and her friends as they nibbled on the leftover food and gossiped about their significant others.

Jill Derbyshire brushed a thin strand of red hair from her eyes and went first, mentioning her husband's prostate: "Ever since his doctor told him it was slightly enlarged the man's been in a state of panic. You know men and their prostates." She rolled her eyes. "Poor baby thinks his sex life is over … I only wish."

On it went, with Cynthia Gladstone talking about how upset

her husband was with his encroaching baldness, and Debbie Stafford mentioning "a boil the size of a small tank" on her husband's butt and his refusing to have it lanced. Denise Gerigk revealed that her husband, Tom, informed that he was inviting kidney disease if he didn't ease up on booze, told his doctor, "Take your diagnosis and shove it where the sun don't shine."

Cathy smiled at the appropriate times, nodded her head, even laughed when the others laughed. She was well aware of the idiosyncrasies of the opposite sex. Usually it would amuse her as much as it did her friends. But a certain dread was setting in. Soon enough she noticed the silence and, even worse, the others were staring at her.

Cathy paused, swallowed once, then feigned surprise. "What?" And she waited. When no one spoke, she continued, trying to put a lighter spin on things. "I have nothing to confess. Frank and I have the perfect marriage. Neither of us complains. We never argue. We don't fight." By exaggerating she figured they'd get the message.

And each woman in turn commiserated, wagging her head in sympathy, the humor in their little gabfest all but gone.

* * *

By the time Cathy returned to Bonita Palms it was almost five o'clock. The bar code affixed to the windshield on the passenger side of her car enabled her to use the special lane designated for residents. The other lane had a guard on duty tending to visitors twenty-four hours a day.

Cathy drove slowly past the rows of palm trees stretching as far as she could see. They lined both sides of the road, in perpendicular lines, as if they'd been planted with meticulous care.

There were no homes to obstruct the view. Those inhabitants who didn't live in one of five condo buildings resided in neighborhoods unto themselves. Each had its own private entrance. Some faced the golf-course; a few fronted one of several man-made lakes. Many were exposed to both.

The names of these communities projected an air of exclusivity. Cathy passed Cozy Hollow, then Doonesbury, followed by Waterford, Royston, and Sleepy Lagoon. Over fifty in all. Some with coach homes or villas, others with larger, freestanding houses. All coming under a set of rules prohibiting any resident from independently adding paint, plantings or decorations that didn't follow strict guidelines.

Cathy occasionally objected to the uniformity, as well as to the unusually high quarterly assessment that was charged by her own community, Augusta. A fee to cover maintenance of the front lawns, repairs to the roadway and roofs, and countless other things that cropped up, predominately in the warm climate of southwest Florida.

She arrived at her circular driveway, remotely opened the garage, drove in, parked, and flicked the closing switch.

In the foyer of her house, she dug her mobile out of her purse, speed-dialed her husband's cell phone. It rang three times then went to voicemail. She didn't bother to leave a message. Frank's so-called "fishing" trips were becoming more frequent of late. She suspected there was something else at play. One of the perils of marrying a man five years her junior, she supposed. But she didn't want to make a fuss; at least not yet.

The antique grandfather clock in the great room chimed the

hour of 5:00 p.m. Cathy didn't hesitate. With purpose she glided into her bathroom, opened the cabinet and removed the small plastic bottle.

"Cylaria," she read off the label. Another pill, this one for her arthritis that had been acting up; the only pill she took before dinner. Its side effects included dry mouth and upset stomach. But prescription medication had become an integral part of her life of late. She was reminded of the pharmaceutical ads on television, how each came with a caveat; or two or three or even ten. Half the time she wondered if the pills were worth the risk.

Cathy shrugged the worry aside. Before going to bed she'd take Crestor to keep her cholesterol under control. In the morning it'd be Micardis for blood pressure and Losec for her stomach. It was what it was. As far as she could tell, her four prescriptions were far below the norm, especially for someone her age. However, she was never one to delude herself. Certain people she knew didn't take pills strictly for medicinal purposes. Eternal youth was their goal, their desire to live longer.

Cathy filled the small glass she kept by the sink with water, popped the pill, and washed it down. Then she undressed and put on one of her favorite silk kimonos she had purchased on a trip to Tokyo a few years back. It was a blend of bright pinks and blues depicting a group of women at market. She stepped into her slippers and proceeded into the kitchen.

Wives with the biggest kitchens cook the least, the popular maxim flashed in her head.

Her kitchen was certainly one of the biggest, painted a neutral color somewhere between beige and white. Of course, she had all the amenities, from jumbo Sub-Zero refrigerator and freezer—both built-in and camouflaged to match the decor—to a stainless-steel double sink, dozens of mahogany cupboards, and a marble table that could seat twelve; all resplendent in the sunlight now streaming through the extra wide skylight that intersected the vaulted ceiling.

Cathy approached the built-in wine cooler that stood next to the butler's pantry and removed one of her favorite Chardonnays. It had a twist top that she preferred over the hassle of a cork. She poured a glass and took a seat in the great room. With Frank away there was no need to cook so she ordered a pizza. Then, cordless phone still in hand, she dialed the familiar number in St. Louis.

When her grandson, Eric, answered, Cathy smiled to herself. The five-year-old liked talking on the telephone.

"Do you know who this is?" she asked.

"Yes."

"What is my name?"

"Grandma."

"That's right, darling. And whom am I speaking to?"

"Hello?"

"Hello, yourself. Can you tell me your name?"

"Hello?"

"Eric—stop saying 'hello.'"

"Goodbye—"

"Wait a minute. Is your mommy home?"

"Hello?"

"Eric!"

"Yes?" He heard his grandmother's raised voice and his own voice softened.

"Go tell your mommy I'd like to have a word with her."

"Hello?"

11

Cathy truly loved her only grandchild, but sometimes he could drive her to distraction. She heard a muffled sound at the other end of the line and then her daughter, Angela's, quick pronouncement: "Sorry, Mom. I'll have to call you back. I've got ten things going on at once."

They said hurried goodbyes and disconnected. Cathy took a sip of wine and frowned. She could picture her daughter's statuesque figure. Brown hair askew. Thirty-six years old but still a kid. Always trying to market one "get rich quick" scheme or another. If it wasn't Isagenix, it was Rodan & Fields skincare, or Açai, the liquid with supposed antioxidant powers. Not that she needed the money; her husband was a lawyer and doing quite well for himself.

But Cathy knew what drove her daughter. She thought back to before Angela was born, when she and Frank could barely make ends meet. Both grew up in St. Louis and came from lower middle-class backgrounds. They'd married at a young age. Cathy worked as a secretary while Frank attended university and studied for his master's degree in business administration. They couldn't afford it but decided to have a baby anyway, and Angela was born. For a year or two the euphoria of being a mother overshadowed the grim reality of their financial situation.

Eventually, however, finding herself without an option, Cathy went back to work, while Frank continued with his schooling during the day. But he soon applied for and was hired as the night manager at an upscale restaurant in the downtown core.

After Frank graduated, he became a partner in the restaurant, then the sole owner. Their fortune turned for the better. One restaurant expanded into two, four, then six.

But all of that came later. Angela grew up with little in the way of fancy clothes or an abundance of toys. There were no day trips to the zoo, no visits to Disneyland. From an early age she'd learned what it was like to go without.

Is it any wonder, Cathy reflected, *that my daughter is obsessed with money?*

She swallowed the last of her wine and poured a refill. She picked up the remote and turned on the seventy-two-inch television. Cathy kicked off her slippers and was just getting comfortable, when the doorbell rang, surprising her…

2

January 5

"What the hell!" I swore.

The phone's insistent chime splintered the bedroom's silence. I brought my arm up until the luminescent dial on my watch came into view: *Not even 6:00 a.m.*

I scrambled to a sitting position, heard a *CLINK* as the base of the phone collided with something. For a moment, I imagined a bottle of Jack Daniels. Then reality set in; it couldn't be Jack, not anymore.

My eyesight adjusted to the dark and I noticed the near empty glass of water.

The phone rang again. I knew it wouldn't be good news. No one called before dawn except when there was trouble. I picked up the receiver, maneuvered it to my ear, and said hello.

"Sheriff?"

Everyone called me sheriff, though in actual fact there was only one who warranted the title, and that was Dean Norman, an elected official. As deputy sheriff I was simply a hired hand.

"Yes?" I said, head still groggy.

"Sorry to bother you. I know how early this is," words rushed. "It's Pedersen."

"I recognized your voice, Brad."

If the sergeant caught the sarcasm, he didn't show it. Instead, he went into a rambling spiel, sentences slurring, state of mind close to panic.

"Whoa," I said, trying to get him to slow down. "Take a deep breath…"

The admonition, spoken in as soothing a voice as I could manage, did the trick.

"There's been a murder, sir."

That got my attention. "Where?"

"At—uh—Bonita Palms."

I came off the bed, stood on not quite awake legs—six foot three and listing—and scratched my mop of grayish-black hair. There'd been so few murders in this part of our territory I could understand the nervousness in Pedersen's voice. "At Bonita Palms?" I echoed.

"Yes, sir. I'm here now. I was the one to take the call. About twenty minutes ago. I … I thought you'd want to know."

"Tell me, Brad, exactly where in Bonita Palms did this alleged murder take place?"

"In a house, sir. In the community of Augusta."

"Augusta?" I needed no reminder that Augusta was one of the most exclusive neighborhoods in the Palms. "Who was it?"

"Cathy Sinclair."

"Mrs. Sinclair?" My skin prickled; I'd known the woman well.

"Yes, sir."

"Did you secure the crime scene?" I said, chiding myself for not asking sooner.

"We did, sir," the sergeant replied. "Scott and I aren't letting anyone in or out." He was referring to Scott Wellington, a corporal on the force.

"Well, you did good then."

"Thank you, sir."

"Keep the perimeter secure. I'm on my way." I disconnected, glanced over at the glass of water and downed what was left.

* * *

I skipped breakfast, shower and shave. Instead, I jumped in my car—a black Chrysler 300—and hit the lights and siren.

The territory of the LCSO, or Lee County Sheriff's Office, encompassed Fort Myers, San Carlos Park, Lehigh Acres, Estero, and Bonita Springs. There were five bureaus. Patrol, Administration, Special Operations, Corrections, and Criminal Investigations. I was in charge of CI.

In the eight years I'd been deputy sheriff, I hadn't seen very many violent crimes. I hoped this wasn't the start of a trend. An unsolved murder would be a major thorn in my side. But the history of Bonita Springs encouraged me. Established in late 1999, the population had grown to over 50,000; split almost equally between men and women, of whom sixty-nine percent were married. I also knew that twenty-one percent were Hispanic, and that the average age fell somewhere in the mid-fifties. This was a laidback community for the most part, more prone to vehicular mishaps than murder.

As I approached my destination, I switched off the siren and flashing lights, and drove into the property.

Stan Beauregard, the head of security at Bonita Palms, was waiting by the main gate. Next to him were his two rent-a-cops—as I liked to call them—Tim Fletcher and Charlie O'Neil. Both men were in their late fifties and had little security experience whatsoever.

Stan himself, a tall, wizened gray-haired man in his sixties, boasted about having once been a policeman somewhere in the Midwest.

All three looked shaken and quite pale. Beauregard took the lead. He explained how the body was found by Mrs. Sinclair's husband, who'd just returned from a fishing trip. "From the doorway it appeared she'd been beaten pretty bad. I didn't want to contaminate the crime scene, so I didn't go inside. C'mon—" he raised the gate arm "we'll head on over there."

I drove through and stopped on the other side. "I'll take it from here, Stan." I didn't have much respect for Beauregard. Not after his background check revealed a few discrepancies in the man's story. But we tolerated each other. I did so out of courtesy; Beauregard out of necessity.

"The husband's at the Gladstone's, right next door," Beauregard offered. "I asked him to wait there until you arrived."

"That's fine," I said. "Thank you for that."

The drive took a little less than ten minutes. I'd been there enough times to know the way. I had to park on the street because the sergeant's and corporal's cars were blocking the entrance to the circular driveway. Both men were in their late thirties and slightly under six feet tall. Brad Pedersen was thin, brown-haired, and fairly good looking. Scott Wellington, on the other hand, was a husky individual with dark hair and a stern face that seldom broke into a smile. The first thing I did, after the men greeted me, was ask them to shut down the flashing lights on their vehicles. "No need to attract any more attention than necessary."

Once the task was completed, I told them to make sure no one left any of the homes in the immediate vicinity, at least not until the occupants could be interviewed. "I'll get you started on that in a few minutes."

Near the front door of the victim's house, I noticed what looked like a business card sticking out of the mailbox. It had been positioned in such a way to make it difficult to miss. The Pizza Hut logo was on the front. The back of the card had a scribbled note about no one answering the bell to accept a delivery. I pocketed the card for a follow-up.

The front door stood partially open. I removed the latex gloves and elasticized booties from my pants pocket and slipped them on. Then I opened the door all the way. There was a great amount of blood, on the walls, the floor, and on the victim herself.

I felt my heart pumping in my chest. I disliked this part of the job. It wasn't that I was squeamish. But I hated to see the depravity that existed, the harm that we did to one another.

I had met Cathy Sinclair on more than one occasion. I'd found her to be the opposite of what one would expect from a woman of her means and stature—down to earth and accommodating. She didn't deserve this.

No one deserved this, I reminded myself.

I approached the victim, took precautions to avoid the blood spatter, bent down and slowly inhaled.

Mrs. Sinclair was wearing a Rolex and that immediately worried me. If this had been a robbery, the perpetrator would have taken the watch. That not being the case changed the dynamic completely.

So, what happened here? I asked myself. I shut my eyes for a moment and allowed the scene to play out in my mind. I imagined the struggle that took place, visualized Mrs. Sinclair being caught off guard, how she must have tried to escape.

I opened my eyes and spotted the pipe wrench. Then the way the woman's arm was twisted in an awkward position. And the deep cut in her neck. I clenched my fists and stood, took one last look at the body, then moved away.

* * *

I became even more concerned while touring the house. Everything was neat and tidy. The windows and doors hadn't been breached. I counted a total of six widescreen television sets in the various rooms, expensive glassware and silverware, and a pair of diamond stud earrings lying on the credenza in the walk-in closet of the master bedroom.

Murder for murder's sake wasn't something to be taken lightly. The task I faced was going to be daunting. Literally hundreds of service people entered the Bonita Palms property each day. The residents made their own decision about who to use for the pool, pest control, garden, air-conditioning, plumbing, electrical work, television repair, and other chores. Tracking these people down and interviewing them would stretch my staff to the limit.

I concluded my search in the oversized garage with a work area occupying the back wall. Everything was immaculately neat and tidy and brand new, like one would find at a hardware store. My eyes skimmed the tools, bench and various implements hanging on hooks from a board above it. One hook was empty.

I returned to the crime scene and examined the pipe wrench lying next to the victim. I was certain it once hung on the now-empty hook in the garage. There was a large smudge of blood running down its length. And something else. A patch of matted hair and probably brain matter. I was certain we wouldn't find any prints. But I'd have forensics give it a thorough going over, nevertheless.

I'd seen enough. I opened the front door and stepped out.

It was still early—not quite 7:15—but the January sun was unusually bright, the sky crystal blue. I found it irreverent, juxtaposed as nature was with the bloodied corpse lying inside.

* * *

Just as I reached the end of the walkway, I noticed a familiar beige Lexus SUV pulling to a stop. The minute the medical examiner of Lee County opened the door I found butterflies fluttering against the wall of my stomach.

Sara Churchill was a blue-eyed blonde. A widow at the age of forty-eight, her husband had been a fireman who was killed on the job.

I said hello, self-conscious about my appearance—no shave or shower. There was no denying my attraction.

"What do we have?" Ms. Churchill asked.

I went into it, described the scene, then offered my deduction that this wasn't a robbery gone bad. "There are no broken locks, no smashed windows. And the murder weapon was left in plain sight." I paused. "Sara—I'm anxious to get your findings."

She looked me straight in the eye. "Relax, Miles. I'll make it a priority. Promise."

* * *

I called my men together and asked them to begin interviewing the neighbors. Then I walked next door and rang the bell. A melodic chime sounded. Less than a minute later I was ushered inside a luxurious house.

The Gladstones had resided in Bonita Palms for five years. Originally from Detroit, they now homesteaded in Florida. Their fortune originated with Paul's side of the family, third-generation owners of a dozen GM car dealerships spread across the state of Michigan. Cynthia wasn't merely good-looking but the opposite of her husband. Paul, at seventy-three, was older by ten years. Short, pot-bellied, and balding. A physically mismatched but popular couple, generous with their time and money, especially at fund-raising events.

Mrs. Gladstone greeted me with grief etched on her face and silently guided me into the great room. Far from a misnomer, the room was of an open concept, with living and dining rooms co-existing. Marble columns rose like Roman arches toward a ceiling that was so high one would have to be an aerialist to change any of the recessed pot lights.

I was familiar with most of the neighborhood homes, but this one stood out. The paintings and sculptures alone were way above my pay-grade. And the drapes and furnishings were of a type I could only admire from a distance.

The victim's husband, Frank Sinclair, was already seated in a high-backed upholstered chair that resembled a wide-bodied throne. I said hello, offered my condolences, and took a seat opposite. Mr. and Mrs. Gladstone had the good sense to leave us alone without my asking.

"I came home early," Sinclair began before I could even ask a question. "I wanted to surprise Cathy. The fish weren't exactly biting but the mosquitoes were. In droves. We'd had enough."

"We?" I questioned.

"Yeah. My usual group. Tim Alonzo, Harry Pringle, and Alan Rheingold. Here—I've written down their names and phone numbers for you."

How convenient, I was thinking as I leaned over and accepted the handwritten note. *What can I expect next*, I wondered, *the name of the perp and his reason for committing the murder?*

I was reminded that I disliked Sinclair from the first time we'd met, years ago. The man was always casual. Too casual. At the moment his tan sport shirt was half unbuttoned; beige shorts, feet sockless in sandals. Sinclair was a young fifty-seven; artificially colored brown hair worn long. His six-foot frame toned and in good shape. And a sing-song voice that was so cheerful it sounded phony.

"I can't believe she's gone," Sinclair was saying, half to himself.

I looked him directly in his eyes. "Do you have any idea who might have done this?"

He didn't flinch. "Me? No. None whatsoever. Everybody loved Cath."

"There was a pipe wrench positioned close to the body. Do you own one?"

"Yes, I do."

No denial … smart move, Frank. "Tell me what happened. You arrived home at what time?"

"Just after five-thirty this morning."

"And you saw what?"

"Nothing at first. I drove into the garage, parked, and headed into the house. I tried to make as little noise as possible, figuring my wife would be asleep. I was tiptoeing past the entranceway when I saw her." Sinclair shook his head. "I ... still can't believe it."

Finally, some emotion out of him, I was thinking. But in a large percentage of these cases, the spouse ended up being the guilty party. I couldn't ignore that fact, even though Sinclair had an alibi that three men would likely back up.

"When did you and your friends leave on your trip?" I asked.

"On the second. We started doing this every two or three months."

"How long a drive is it?"

"Four hours. Northeast of Tampa."

"What hotel did you stay at?"

"We didn't. We found a private home through Airbnb instead."

"I'll need the exact address."

"Of course."

I kept at it for another half-hour, figuring if I caught the man lying about the smallest, most insignificant detail, everything else might unravel. But his story held. Or at least it did on the surface. I'd have to contact his friends, see if their statements of events matched Frank Sinclair's, though I suspected they would.

I stood and again told him I was sorry for his loss, then added, "I take it you have no plans for immediate travel?"

He shot a look at me that said, *I know darn well why you're asking that stupid question.* "No plans whatsoever."

* * *

I drove directly to a narrow red-bricked building in the heart of downtown Fort Myers. The current sheriff's office was being renovated so we were allotted this space in the interim. Luckily, the room I was given was above average; I could meet with a dozen people comfortably should the need arise. The downside was the lack of windows and fluorescent lighting that didn't make up for the difference.

Before I could get comfortable at my desk, I received consecutive phone calls. First from the mayor of Fort Myers, then the mayor of Bonita Springs. Each expressed concern about the murder and asked what I planned to do about it. I wanted to tell them it was none of their damn business; but common sense prevailed, and I assured both that no stone would be left unturned.

By the time I opened an electronic file on the woman's murder, however, I was pissed at my holding back. It rankled that men supposedly as astute as both mayors wouldn't comprehend the complexity of the situation, would not understand the quandary I faced.

Screw them, an inner voice counseled. *Just get on with the job.*

I began by entering my notes into the computer—what I'd found in the house, the condition of the corpse, the murder weapon, my interview with the deceased's husband. Midmorning Stan Beauregard delivered the list of visitors for the past week, as well as the service people approved for entrance to the Bonita Palms property. There were over six hundred names in all.

Lunch was a Big Mac at the nearby McDonalds.

By late afternoon, I'd completed lengthy discussions with Brad Pedersen and Scott Wellington. Their interviews with the Sinclair neighbors in Augusta had gone as expected. No one had seen or heard anything. The subdivision was more or less isolated.

I looked at my watch—past 6:00 p.m. I'd had enough. Time to go home. I envisioned a tall JD on the rocks; maybe more than one. Then I chastised myself.

The drive took me east of 75 to a fairly new, un-gated subdivision off Corkscrew Road. They were small homes, nothing deluxe. Mine had two bedrooms and two baths, kitchen and great room, if one could call it that. A total of fifteen hundred square feet in all, decorated conservatively. A few framed photographs of me in my younger days; one on a golf course, another on a fishing boat.

By the time I'd undressed, washed, and stashed my gun away, I was more than ready for a touch of Jack. I stepped up to the empty liquor cabinet in the great room, imagined it still being stocked with my favorite beverage … and paused.

Promises made. Promises broken. I realized I couldn't go on this way. My troubles were supposedly behind me. If I slipped there'd be no going back. It would be okay if I could stop at one drink, but not a chance.

I pushed myself away from the cabinet and walked into the master bathroom. My Crestor medication was sitting on the counter. I partially filled a glass with water, popped one of the pills and swallowed. Then I opened the drawer beneath the mirror and removed the container of Narvia. This prescription was my magic elixir, used to control anxiety. More than that, it dimmed my need for alcohol by helping me to unwind. I shook out two pills and washed them down.

Back in the great room, I noticed the tremor in my fingers as I raised my hands to my face and rubbed my eyes. Memories of the past wouldn't leave me. Too much had transpired. Too much regret. Before long, my head started spinning.

3

Late evening

I knew my name and age: Miles Delany, fifty-three. And I believed my description was fairly accurate: 6' 1", 227 pounds, blackish hair, hazel eyes.

Everything else was a blur. I had no idea of time or place. No idea of where I was. And no idea how I got here. I remembered parking my car in front of a bar with a half-lit neon sign above the door.

The neighborhood was seedy but bustling. Dozens of people mingled, predominantly men in their twenties and thirties, with the occasional teen thrown in the mix for good measure. Many held bottles of beer or liquor; some openly toked on joints; a few of the women laughed too loudly.

I walked among them, feeling far too old for this crowd. Maui Jim sunglasses shaded my eyes; a blue Dolphins cap positioned low over my forehead.

This particular street was narrow, with few spots where I could pass without being bumped. There were no "Excuse me's."

People jostled each other and I went with the flow. But when a heavily built, mustached man in his mid-thirties, scowl on his face, came too close, I was ready for him. I made sure our shoulders connected.

The man swore at me, aimed his fist at my ribcage.

Somehow, I hadn't lost my dexterity. My turn was slower than usual but quick enough to avoid contact. The fist passed harmlessly to the side.

The man tried coming at me again.

A voice in my head urged me on. I threw an uppercut that clipped the man's chin, sending him crumbling to the ground.

Which was when his friends approached.

I counted four of them; or what appeared to be four. My focus was off at the moment so I couldn't say for sure. But they were all athletic looking. Not a wuss in the bunch; overconfident enough to believe in the odds.

They took the classic approach: one in front, one in back, and one on each side.

It became a flurry of punches and kicks. I knew I shouldn't be enjoying this, but I was. And I gave as good as I got; blackening eyes, breaking teeth. Not that I was eluding punishment myself. Some of what I absorbed was truly painful. But even that wouldn't have stopped me. It took the sound of a siren in the distance to make me realize the folly of my game.

As I started to back off, I heard my assailants taunting me.

"Where you goin', chicken-shit?"

"Pussy can't take the heat?"

"Runnin' home to momma?"

I paused. *Stay or go?*

Finally, I flipped them off and bolted. But I had no idea how I found my car. No recollection of driving home.

* * *

Sleep was elusive. When it came, the dreams were troubled. Images flashed then dissolved: men with clenched fists, arms flashing, punches missing, punches connecting. Violence for violence 's sake.

I awoke early the next morning, fully dressed in last night's clothes, feeling soreness in both hands. I looked in the bathroom mirror and froze, disbelieving what I was seeing. I'd been fantasizing. That's all it was, a fantasy, right? My imagination had involved me in a situation that went against my nature. It couldn't have been anything else.

I unbuttoned my shirt. Something was wrong here. Numerous bruises peppered my body. If this had all been a fantasy, how could I explain that, along with my swollen knuckles?

4

January 7

Frank Sinclair stood in the bathroom, looking down with disgust as he tried to coax the urine to flow. He gave it his utmost concentration. He cursed and stroked until, at last, an unstable stream began to trickle. A portion splattered the lip of the toilet bowl. Then he noticed the backsplash on the floor and swore to himself. Various prostate examines all proved he was healthy; though peeing still remained a challenge. He was told there was a pill that could help but it'd likely mess with his libido. This was a risk Frank wasn't willing to take.

He took hold of his penis and examined it. Was the damn thing getting smaller? His doctor had confirmed in a recent visit that his body was changing. He was gaining weight and losing height. It probably made sense that his penis would shrink as well.

He washed his hands and finger-combed his hair, then paused. The artificial color his hair stylist applied every five weeks or so was adequate; not overdone. Light brown with just enough trace of gray along the sides.

He smiled at what he saw in the mirror. For some reason the short-sleeved, half-unbuttoned pink shirt he was wearing amused him. That, and his lime-green shorts. In another era he would've made the perfect hippie.

He reached into his pocket and removed a Viagra tablet in a single foil wrap. *Why carry a full sleeve when only one Viagra's necessary?* he was thinking.

Actually, not necessary at all, he acknowledged. But lately he'd gotten into the habit of popping the pill before each of his dalliances, simply to be on the safe side. He'd never been accused of failing to please. But ever since his prostate enlarged, he didn't want to take the chance on performing inadequately and being embarrassed.

* * *

Barbara Miller, tall and thin, with long black hair and wide enticing eyes of a provocative nature, was lying naked beneath the covers of the king-size bed in the master bedroom, wondering what was taking Frank so long.

She knew that under the circumstances—so close to the murder of Frank's wife, one of her best friends—she should've canceled today. But Frank had insisted, using the argument that breaking with their monthly tradition would throw their karma off for good.

So here she was. And if the truth were known, that tingle was back; she felt it beneath her skin. A sly teasing that rose from her loins and threatened to turn her brain into mush.

Her monthly "lunches" with Frank, for over a year, had given Barbara a purpose. The simplest show of affection, from either sex, had always turned her on. Frank filled a void that she felt was lacking.

Barbara's husband, Bill, was nineteen years her senior. They'd met in his accounting office in Buffalo, New York. She was a registered nurse at the time, hired by Bill's insurance company to handle his annual examination.

It wasn't love at first sight; nor was there a physical attraction on her part. But a few dates for a harmless coffee led to a harmless lunch, which led to a harmless dinner. Things multiplied from there until it was harmless no longer.

Bill had been married for thirty-two years but promised to leave his wife. Barbara wasn't involved with anyone, having broken up with her boyfriend half a year previously.

He proposed a month after his divorce finalized and Barbara accepted. Their first years together were more tolerable than unique. Then Bill retired and insisted they move to Florida. His health issues began soon afterwards, and Barbara grew bored.

A neighbor suggested she try real estate. Once into it, Barbara knew she'd found her calling. An added bonus was the empty homes she had access to, many of them completely furnished.

Her trysts with both men and women were kept discreet. Most were one-night stands—until Frank. Thanks to her newfound career, there was no need for a hotel. Her affair with him continued in relative comfort and seclusion.

* * *

"Ta-ta!"

Barbara looked up, amused by a beaming Frank standing in

front of her. His arms were spread above his head, his shirt half open, the zipper on his shorts undone.

She stopped him before he could fully undress. "Here—let me help you with that." She came off the bed.

Frank placed his hands on her shoulders and coaxed her closer.

Barbara noticed his grin turning lecherous and almost gave herself to him then and there. Instead, forcing her concentration, she helped him out of his shirt, then placed her palm on the fly of his shorts. "My, my, my," she said playfully. "Wee Willie is growing."

Frank placed a gentle hand between her legs.

The least contact, as usual, was enough to send Barbara soaring. She moved quicker, removed Frank's shorts, then his underwear. His penis sprung loose, pointing skyward. She ran her fingers up and down its shaft.

"It would behoove you to let loose," she joked.

Frank trapped Barbara between his body and the mattress, thrust out his pelvis until she tumbled backward onto the bed. She went to pull him on top of her, but Frank had something else in mind.

His mouth between her legs sent Barbara into ecstasy. She moaned, then cried out. She arched her back and shuddered, not wanting anything more than to feel what she was experiencing at the moment. Her imagination soared. She implored Frank to continue, calling him "baby" and "sweetie," but hardly aware of the words she was using.

Frank rose above her, cupped the back of her neck, and brought his face close. Their lips met; she opened her mouth and French kissed him. Barbara found she wanted more, reached down, being willful but not caring. She guided his penis inside, clamped her eyes shut, and waited for Frank's thrusts to match her own.

Then, determined, Barbara stilled her body.

Frank pulled free and asked, "What's wrong?"

She wanted to tell him but was unable to say it aloud.

"Barbara?"

She hesitated, a hint of lasciviousness in her eyes.

"What is it?"

She whispered in his ear.

Frank shrugged, waited to see if she was serious.

She nodded once, a flush reddening her cheeks.

Frank changed positions.

His penis entered her mouth and Barbara found all extraneous sound coming to an end. As she sucked, she felt she was tasting her own essence, as if having sex with herself. And she needed it, *craved* it.

Frank followed her instructions of a minute ago. He pulled out of her mouth, lowered himself, reentered her vagina.

Barbara lost count of the number of times he exchanged places, from bottom to top and back again. The sublime taste on her lips was soon matched by what she was feeling below. And she was struck by this visceral sense of pleasure she couldn't describe. She wanted it to go on forever.

5

Bill Miller—balding and rail-thin, a mere shell of his former self—was seated nearby in his car, a one-year-old Bentley with 3,347 miles on the odometer.

He'd seen his wife enter the house over an hour ago. Frank Sinclair had followed her in not long afterwards. Bill had fostered suspicions for a long while. He now had it confirmed and it angered him in the worst way.

He sat up straighter and conjured up old memories. *What had I been? All of twenty-five at the time?* Too young to be married, even if Ruthanne was his childhood sweetheart. Too young and too foolish.

* * *

Bill's parents paid for his schooling. He graduated from University of Buffalo with a degree in accounting. He was expected to join the family's well-established firm in his hometown. But Bill declined, alienating his father.

Ruthanne became pregnant and they eloped. Bill soon felt

trapped. A friend invited him to join his business, servicing soup aisles of the large retail chains, with a great deal of travel across the northeast. This was the precise opportunity Bill had been looking for.

A girl in every port wasn't a cliché. Bill not only had his looks back then, but charisma and the gift of gab. The thought of having sex with a total stranger had always been tantalizing to Bill. More and more he anticipated that first kiss, the first reveal of a naked breast.

Ruthanne's pregnancy caused her to put on quite a bit of weight. Bill often compared the lithe bodies of his one-night stands to that of his corpulent wife.

His son, Jonathan, was born, and for a time Bill acted like a normal father. He cut back on some of his travel. But he didn't lift a finger to help at home. Ruthanne fed their son and changed his diapers, tended to his tantrums, his multiple coughs and colds.

Bill couldn't wait to get back on the road. He could no longer deny that his craving for sex was insatiable. From Boston to Pittsburg, Philadelphia to New York. There wasn't a woman he met who he didn't want to bed.

Making love to Ruthanne became a chore. She got pregnant a second time and Bill was upset with himself. By the time Gary was born, his escapades had become so convoluted he lost track of which girl, in what city, he'd been with last.

His travels would have continued had his father not put additional pressure on him to join the family firm once and for all. But remaining in Buffalo didn't stop Bill from lusting after an entire new group of women: barmaids and waitresses, even secretaries in his office.

Meanwhile, Ruthanne was taking better care of herself. Her weight was back to normal and she'd regained a sense of style.

Bill didn't change. Not until his sons were graduating high school, followed by university. Which was when guilt finally manifested itself and he came to understand that something profound was lacking in his life. He didn't know if he was capable of being faithful, but he wanted to try. He stopped his sexual dalliances cold turkey and paid more attention to his wife.

Her reaction wasn't what he expected; she was aloof. Whenever he took her to dinner, her silence in the restaurant was magnified by the noisy chatter around them. He'd go to touch her and she'd pull away. Finally, Ruthanne asked for a divorce.

Bill continued to live at home, though he realized he wasn't wanted. Barbara entered the picture and he was primed and ready. His sole objective was to pursue and win her over. He talked about divorcing his wife as if this would be a sacrifice, and not something into which he was being pressured.

He was persistent. As soon as his split from Ruthanne was finalized, he formally proposed. It felt strange being married to another woman, but he remained faithful.

Bill retired at the age of sixty-six and the move to Florida followed. His home in Bonita Palms cost upwards of five million dollars. In less than a year he had difficulty maintaining an erection. He visited one specialist after the other and tried numerous solutions. The Viagra experience lasted six months; the daily use of Cialis a few months longer. From there he went to pumps to rings to naturopathic cures. Nothing worked.

Bill found it ironic: he was committed to having a monogamous relationship for the first time in his life. Instead of reaping the benefit, it had become a curse.

* * *

Bill started the car but waited, taking a last look at the house. He pictured his wife and Frank Sinclair in bed, bumping thighs. He could imagine the sounds they were making, could practically inhale their secretions.

It took eight minutes to arrive at his address in Augusta. A long driveway led to a multi-car garage. Bill activated the door and parked.

His home office was spacious and brightly lit. Twenty by thirty, with a built-in library running the length of the far wall. He took a seat at his mahogany desk, removed a pill from a container he kept in the top drawer, put it in his mouth and dry swallowed. Celenome was his stomach cancer medication. Bill had revealed his disease to no one, especially Barbara. He wasn't being magnanimous or selfless. He simply knew that she wouldn't care one way or the other.

But it wasn't his physical problems that occupied Bill's mind at the moment. His finances had begun a serious decline nearly two years ago. Bad investments coupled with greed. Whatever he tried had failed to pay off. Solid tips became dangerous pratfalls. People he always listened to were no longer trustworthy. His portfolio had shrunk by several million dollars.

Bill did what he figured any other red-blooded American would do. He was facing financial ruin, so he began a second career. The easy part was getting his friends and neighbors to trust him. He'd always been creative; it took a bit more time to decide what scheme to use.

He called it The Bill Miller Fund and promoted it by arguing that inflation was once again around the corner. The U.S. dollar was going to fall. His fund promised to buy an unspecified commodity at an unspecified price at some unspecified future point in time. Bill gained the trust of his clients by explaining that commodity prices didn't always go up but fluctuated. His fund would take long or short positions to hedge against these swings.

The commodity of choice, in Bill's case, was oil, especially with the universal price being deflated. He ascertained that a contract covering an amount of a thousand barrels, for instance, would solely require a deposit of five to ten percent, enabling him to use ninety to ninety-five percent of the invested money for his own use.

However, not being wedded to correct ethical, fiduciary and regulatory principles, Bill decided to not risk any of his own cash. After all, he had a comfortable lifestyle to support. To keep people at bay and avoid suspicion, he made sure to pay out modest "returns" at the end of each month. Meanwhile, his clients were on the hook for millions of dollars.

Bill smiled at the thought as he pulled out a key from his pants pocket and unlocked the top drawer of his desk. How perfect that Frank Sinclair was one of his largest investors. Bill removed Frank's file and relocked the drawer.

A feeling of satisfaction came over him, knowing that he was going to do to Frank ... *Exactly what the sonofabitch is doing to my wife.*

6

January 17

The memorial service for Cathy Sinclair was being held in a private function room at the Bonita Palms clubhouse, three o'clock in the afternoon. I made sure to arrive early so I wouldn't miss anyone. My investigation into Mrs. Sinclair's death was going nowhere. Forensics confirmed that her murder was caused by blunt force trauma to the head. The weapon was indeed her husband's wrench left at the crime scene. Why it was used and how it came into the hands of the doer remained a puzzle.

The room I'd just entered was golf-club chic, meaning it had little to recommend it. Twenty-four by thirty-six. White walls and ceiling. Large color portraits of Tiger Woods, Jack Nicklaus and the late Arnold Palmer on display. Upholstered chairs were scattered around the room with dozens of flower arrangements placed in-between.

Tables in two of the four corners were loaded with hors d'oeuvres. An open bar was set up in the third corner. I stepped up to it and ordered a Diet Coke. The bartender was a bespectacled young man in his mid twenties. I accepted my drink in a tall glass with ice, left a dollar tip, and walked away.

I circled the outer perimeter of the room, taking note of the individual floral pieces and the cards of sympathy attached to each one. I didn't feel conspicuous because, other than the bartender and a woman from the club who was acting as hostess, I was still the only guest in attendance.

I noticed the Sony electronic video display sitting on a table by itself in the fourth corner. Photos of Cathy Sinclair played in a continuous loop. Cathy and her husband in various poses. Cathy in tennis and golf attire. Multiple photos of the woman with her daughter and grandson.

I reflected on why the memorial was being held here in the first place: The penalty one paid for having two homes. Most of the Sinclair family resided in St. Louis. It made sense to hold the funeral in Cathy's Midwestern town—which took place almost a week ago—and the memorial service here in Florida.

Money can complicate matters, I was concluding just as footsteps in the hallway drew my attention. I wondered who'd be first to pay their respects. Would it be Cathy's husband, whom I thought would have—make that *should* have—been here by now? Or one of her good friends?

I took a sip from my glass and waited.

Frank Sinclair bounded into the room with a surprisingly spry step. I caught his nod as he acknowledged me. Then I watched him glide up to the bar.

What a perfect suspect he makes, even with a solid alibi, I figured. But before I could take that thought any further, I was greeted by Tom and Denise Gerigk. I shook their hands and offered my condolences. I liked the couple, though something told me that a German Canadian married to a French Canadian would eventually lead to a volatile relationship.

"Sheriff—" someone said at my back and I turned.

Debbie Stafford was smiling. Or what she must have thought passed for a smile. The overweight woman was a puzzle to me. At the moment she was hanging on to her husband, Larry, as if she hadn't a care in the world. But I knew better, having been called to her house a few too many times; imagined ghosts lurking in the dark.

"Mr. and Mrs. Stafford," I found myself saying in a muted voice, "I'm sorry for the loss of your friend."

They'd no sooner left my side when Jack and Jill Derbyshire said hello, followed almost immediately by Paul and Cynthia Gladstone.

I took a last sip of my Diet Coke and returned the empty glass to the bar. The room was filling up. I'd come here today to pay my respects as well as to eyeball anyone who might arouse suspicion. *Based on crime scene evidence, Mrs. Sinclair knew her killer. It could very well be one of her neighbors or friends.*

I checked the time. I'd promised to meet the medical examiner in less than two hours for an early dinner. I'd finally worked up enough nerve to ask Sara Churchill out. I was surprised when she accepted my invitation. Though, at the moment, I was growing apprehensive. It'd been a long while since I'd dated anyone and was risking I'd make a fool of myself.

My gaze shifted without conscious intent. Sure enough, my eyes made the connection before my brain could register what I was seeing.

Half in and half out of the corridor, Frank Sinclair and

Barbara Miller were huddled together. They weren't touching but their body language spoke volumes all the same. Something in their eyes fueled my suspicion. I figured on a prurient history between the two.

I removed a notepad from my breast jacket pocket and scribbled down both their names, followed by a question mark. *Something's going on between these two, and I'll need to find out exactly what's what.*

* * *

Roy's in Bonita Springs wasn't the kind of restaurant I could afford on a regular basis. But I wanted to impress Ms. Churchill. So here I was, feeling like a school kid, my mind unable to focus.

Even though it was early the restaurant was busy as usual. The lighting was on the bright side. Every seat at the liquor bar near the front was occupied, as were those at the food bar next to it. The main room, where I was seated, had a high ceiling with a few decorative pieces on the walls, mainly photographs of girls or flowers with a Hawaiian flare.

I'd been given a corner table, yet the noise level was still at a higher than normal decibel. The clientele all looked content; smiling, eating, talking. There didn't appear to be a troubled or disgruntled man or woman in the bunch.

Affluence embodied Bonita Springs, as I well knew. More than a few of the residents could buy and sell me many times over. Why, even the tourists gave the impression of being well off.

"Excuse me," the waitress said, a cute twenty-something, "your Diet Coke, Sheriff."

I waited until she placed the drink in front of me and left. Then I asked myself how she knew who I was. Did I have a neon sign that announced my vocation?

"Well, hello," I heard Sara Churchill say before I even noticed her. "Nice to see you away from work."

I'd forgotten about her sensual voice. "It *is* nice," I said. "Thanks for joining me."

"It's my pleasure." She took her seat.

"Drink?"

"What are you having?"

"Diet Coke."

"Oh," she said as if it wasn't what she expected of me. "Do you mind if I have a drink-drink?"

"I don't mind at all. What'll it be?"

"Umm. How about a Gray Goose Martini?"

"Straight up? Olive?"

"How'd you know?"

"Instinct," I said and smiled. I was about to search out the waitress when she appeared as if somehow cognizant of my need. I placed the order, then brought my attention back to Sara. Her blonde hair was accented by the mauve, silk dress she was wearing, semi-low cut with a dash of cleavage.

"Any progress on the Sinclair case?" she asked.

"Something about the husband, Frank, still rubs me the wrong way," I offered, interested in her take.

"I thought his friends vouched for him?"

"They did. But…"

"But what?"

"Look—the wrench was his, of that there's no doubt. And it isn't likely Cathy was using it at the time she was murdered.

Several of her friends told me she'd never try to fix something herself. And records show neither she nor Frank called for a repairman. Nor would they have intentionally left it lying around in the foyer. So how else did it get into the killer's hands, unless the killer was her husband?"

"And if it wasn't?"

"Then I have no idea. All I can tell you is that it wasn't a random stranger. Mrs. Sinclair opened the door for her assailant. There was no forced entry. It's ... frustrating as hell. And I'm far from making an arrest."

She fake-frowned. "I'm sure Mayor Hillier is pleased."

I laughed. "The man is a piece of work, isn't he? Not an hour goes by when he isn't on the phone harassing me."

"So, tell him to get lost."

"I'm about ready to do so."

"He does the same to me."

"He does?" I was surprised. It wasn't the medical examiner's responsibility to search out suspects, or to answer to the mayor. "What does he expect of you? That you'll get the cadaver to reveal the truth about what happened?"

"Something like that," Sara said just as her drink arrived.

"Well," I held up my glass in a toast, "here's to solving the murder sooner than later."

We clinked, then drank.

Sara used a spoon to gather a portion of the edamame that was sitting on a plate on the table. I wasn't a fan so left it all to her. Then I asked why in the world she'd choose a mostly male-dominated profession.

"I followed in my mother's footsteps," she said. "As a matter of fact, I'm the third in the Churchill family. All women. There was my great grandmother, my mother, then me. Only one generation was skipped."

I studied her as she talked, again admiring the throatiness of her voice. I picked up the menu and pretended to study it while cautioning myself not to say or do anything stupid.

"What's so interesting in there?" Sara inquired, smiling.

I shrugged. "Lots of things. Have you eaten here before?"

"Uh-uh. But I've wanted to. Why don't you order for both of us?"

I liked that she trusted me. I placed our order: salads and Roy's Trio, one of the restaurant's signature dishes.

For the next little while we talked shop until our salads arrived. Then I caught the way Sara was holding her fork, in her fist instead of her fingers. In an effort to be playful I imitated her. Sara put her fork down, her expression turning serious. I cursed my boldness, especially with someone I hardly knew.

Then Sara burst out laughing. "If you must know, my brother got me into this habit when I was a kid. It's something I've never been able to shake."

"Oh," I said nonchalantly, "what habit is that?"

"Very funny." She picked up her fork and tried holding it the normal way. It fell to the table. "See what I mean?"

By the time the main course was served, Sara was halfway through her glass of wine. After a few mouthfuls, she was praising the food when my cell went off.

I left the phone in my jacket pocket. "It'll stop."

"Hey—it doesn't bother me. It could be work related. Maybe you should take it?"

"Uh-uh." The evening was going so well I was afraid of spoiling it.

I asked Sara if she grew up in southwest Florida.

"I did. Born and bred here, as they say."

"Mmm. One of the few."

"That's true. Not too many of us natives around."

The waitress brought menus for dessert. Before we could make our choices, my cell rang again. I was vacillating between answering and letting it go to voicemail, when it stopped.

I selected the macadamia nut tart while Sara chose the sorbet trio. We each ordered a decaf cappuccino.

My attention was drawn to the table next to us. A teenage boy was celebrating his birthday. One of the wait-staff was snapping his picture as he blew out the candle in a hot fudge brownie. I couldn't help but reflect on my own son, now deceased, and his turbulent years growing up.

I was turning back to Sara when my phone rang a third time. Concern got the better of me. I pulled it out of my pocket and said hello.

"Sheriff—it's Brad. There's been another one."

For a moment, I didn't quite grasp the meaning of what I was being told. "Another what?"

"Another murder, sir. At Bonita Palms."

7

Three hours earlier

Debbie and Larry Stafford drove home in silence from Cathy Sinclair's memorial service. The January weather remained above normal, though the sea breeze had dropped the late afternoon temperature to the low sixties.

Larry parked his 7-series BMW in the garage and entered the house. He stepped into his office after passing through a wide hallway lined with equestrian memorabilia that spoke volumes about his wife's vocation.

Frederick Farms had been one of the most successful and prestigious racehorse breeders in Kentucky. The farm had recently been sold, leaving the family—Debbie, along with her brother and sister—with mega-millions.

Larry didn't begrudge Debbie her inheritance. He himself had had a fine career as a real estate lawyer. His only regret was not having children. Debbie had been against it and he couldn't change her mind. And now they were facing turbulent times. He and Debbie had been married for almost forty years, the first thirty-nine of which had passed in relative calm. Almost a year ago, however, things started to change.

It began with his wife's weight. It'd always been above normal but now it was ballooning out of control. The more she ate the more miserable she became. When she wasn't eating, she was praying. When she wasn't praying, she was hearing voices. Every suggestion Larry made—from updating her prescription medication to seeking professional help—fell on deaf ears.

A wood plaque of Jesus was attached to the wall by his office door. Over twenty crosses and crucifixes were scattered throughout the house. If that wasn't overkill, Larry didn't know what was.

Debbie had become maniacal lately, experimenting with hormone replacement therapy, then colonic irrigation, and was ready for whatever next came off the internet. Her eagerness to share her "cures" with anyone who'd listen embarrassed Larry to no end.

Tonight, he knew if he stayed home for dinner he'd get into another endless argument. He simply wasn't in a mood for it. Larry grabbed his car keys, called to his wife over his shoulder, "I'm going out," and quickly left.

* * *

Debbie waited for the garage door to shut before exiting the bedroom. She once loved her husband, but for some reason they were growing further and further apart. She blamed Larry for it; every little thing she did lately stirred the hackles between them. She could no longer confide in him. Larry wasn't the empathetic partner he'd once been.

Debbie was wearing a cotton sundress without shoes. She'd

removed her makeup, pantyhose, and jewelry a short while ago. She walked into the kitchen, opened the fridge, and took hold of the Saran-wrapped aluminum container of strawberry cheesecake; her favorite. Rather than cut a portion and serve it on a plate, she picked out a fork from the drawer, took a seat at the table, and gorged.

Halfway through, the tears started to flow. Debbie made no attempt to wipe them away.

She had no idea why she was crying; these bouts just came upon her. One minute she'd be perfectly happy; the next she'd feel this anvil upon her shoulders, as if her world was caving in and there was nothing she could do about it.

She finished the pie, stood and walked into the bathroom. It was big, like the rest of the house. Six bedrooms, a massive great room, an L-shaped kitchen.

Debbie peered into the mirror. *What am I? A good fifty-something pounds above normal for a woman my age and height?* It didn't matter. She'd inherited her father's genes. As her momma used to say—and apropos of someone in their business—nothing wrong with being as big and strong as a horse.

But there *was* more than one thing wrong with her. She took Meaford for the ache in her joints, Cymore for hypertension, and more recently Narvia for her escalating anxiety. She grabbed the plastic container sitting on the counter and removed one of the white pills. Then, worried it wouldn't be sufficient, she placed a second one in her mouth, put a half-full bottle of water to her lips, and took six, slow sips. It was never five or seven—always six.

She leaned closer to the mirror and admired the whiteness of her teeth. Her best feature as far as she was concerned. She parted her lips, then stuck out her tongue. She bit down ... hard. Then twice more ... until she could feel a slow trickle of blood.

She paused and closed her eyes. The tangy taste on her lips was better than anything she could imagine.

* * *

Five o'clock and Debbie found she couldn't keep the thoughts straight in her head. If someone asked what had transpired in the last while, she didn't think she'd be able to answer.

She went to her private room as if she had no choice, opened the door and stepped inside. It was of average size, ten feet by ten feet. Desk with computer and a swivel chair. A message board hanging on the wall with a pinned to-do list. Forty-eight-inch television off to one side, with an ironing board and iron positioned in front of it. A floor to ceiling bookcase lined the entire back wall; containing a couple hundred books, most of a religious, occult, and self-help nature.

The Bible Debbie now took in hand concealed a switch that she activated. The bookcase split apart revealing a secret alcove six feet deep. The original owner of the house, a semi-famous novelist, married with four hyperactive kids, had built the room to give him the peace and quiet he needed to do his work. Other than painting it stark white, Debbie had left the alcove empty until a year ago when her religious obsession took hold and she went on a buying spree. A heavy, carved-wood statue of Christ nailed to the cross, four feet tall, stood next to a brilliantly lit alter in red. Everything had been purchased at an auction when the fifty-year-old neighborhood church had closed for good.

She approached the alter and paused. Debbie shut her eyes,

brought her palms together and began to pray. Visits to the secret prayer room had always given her comfort. And this was what she needed once again.

All was peaceful. At first. Until she heard a distinct whisper and her eyes flew open. *What's that?*

Debbie looked left and right, trying to determine where the voice was coming from. Was it Jesus on the cross? Inside her own head? Or one of her ghosts?

8

8:32 P.M.

Instead of ringing the bell, I knocked on the door. It felt like yesterday that I'd been here, interviewing Cathy Sinclair's husband. Her closest neighbors, the Gladstones, were good people. They'd been living the kind of retirement most of us would envy. And now that life had been shattered.

Paul Gladstone opened the door and wordlessly beckoned me inside.

I was taken aback by the change in Cynthia's husband. The man had always looked his age of seventy-three, but tonight he'd been transformed into someone much older. His posture was stooped. His potbelly not only protruded, it sagged over his belt buckle. What little was left of his gray hair was in disarray. And his eyes—always projecting warmth—were puffy and red, burning with a hurt so obvious it was disquieting.

"Her body's in there," he said, his voice all but a whisper.

I followed where he was pointing and headed along the hallway to the kitchen, where I acknowledged my second in command, Brad Pedersen, then several of the technicians who were already at work. The medical examiner hadn't yet arrived. Sara and I had decided in the restaurant that it'd be best if I preceded her to the crime scene.

The kitchen was large enough for us all to fit comfortably. It had every amenity imaginable, from extra wide fridge, to built-in barbecue, butler's pantry and double sink. There was a modern design to it that'd make any woman proud.

Mrs. Gladstone's body lay on the tiled floor, her skin already drained of color. The apparent murder weapon—a bronze statue belonging to the victim and her husband—was lying next to her. Cynthia's face was compressed; her cheeks were drawn, making them look more skeletal than human. Her head had been crushed so viciously, pieces of skull were jutting out.

Brad Pedersen explained: "Her husband called it in. He'd been out running a few errands and had just returned home." He paused. "Man-oh-man, it's one thing to deal with the Sinclair homicide … but two murders in Bonita Palms in less than two weeks?"

My own sentiment exactly. "Two murders and two different weapons used." *This makes it far less likely that Frank Sinclair is the culprit.* "Did you get a fix on the time?"

Pedersen nodded. "Mr. Gladstone was gone for an hour and forty-five minutes. So somewhere between 5:30 and 7:15."

I pictured Cynthia Gladstone relaxing at home, perhaps reading a book or watching television … until she's interrupted by a neighbor or a friend, or at least someone she knew.

"Any sign of a break-in?" I asked, already knowing the answer.

"Her husband claims everything was normal. First thing I did was check the doors, windows, and garage."

"Did they keep the front door locked?"

"Always. But the alarm's solely activated when they go to bed at night. Haven't had a problem in the fourteen years they've been living here."

I lowered my voice. "What do you make of it, Brad?"

There was no hesitation. "Different weapons but the same M.O. Too early to be a copycat killing."

I agreed. *Two victims, one killer. Unless we catch him soon, this is plainly going to escalate.*

* * *

The minute Sara's SUV pulled up I headed outside. There was no regulation at work against us dating but we both felt it was far too soon for anyone to know about it. Meanwhile, despite our evening being interrupted, I was certain something had clicked between us and I was anxious to see how it would play out.

I gave Sara a brief wave then went to check the perimeter of the house. The property in back was two lots in one and accessible from both sides. There was grass instead of a paved pathway; the landscaping so pristine it made me feel intrusive.

Unlike the neighboring homes, the lanai wasn't enclosed by a wire screen. It sat in the open: fair-sized swimming pool surrounded by a full outdoor kitchen, patio furniture in bright summer colors, and a gas barbecue. The tiled area was extensive and gave way to a manicured lawn with an impressive variety of flowerbeds, from Lilies of the Nile, to petunias and marigolds.

I headed to the edge of the property where I paused and looked back. The moon was full. Solar-powered decorative lights lit the ground and made it easy to see for quite a distance. I could make out my own footprints—faint indentations in the grass—but no one else's. I could also see into the great room from where I was standing.

I imagined being an intruder, aiming to enter the house from in back. *But how did I get here? Was I parachuted in? Hop a ride on a drone?*

There was no intruder, I concluded. *No one surprised Mrs. Gladstone.* The only question left was who killed her: A neighbor? A relative or friend? Someone she was comfortable with? A person she trusted? I recognized what I was facing, and I much preferred a madman, a loony-bin escapee, some psychotic bastard.

I let my eyes sweep the property one more time, hoping to spot something I'd missed, a physical clue that would make everything clear. I didn't want to rush, but after fifteen minutes I'd had enough, figuring there was nothing more to be gained out here.

I headed back inside, said goodbye to Sara, then instructed Brad Pedersen to let me know when everything was wrapped up.

* * *

I was almost at my office when I answered a call from Sheriff Dean Norman. In the beginning we spoke often, usually two or three times a day. But the closer the sheriff got to his retirement, scheduled for late April, the more disinterested he appeared to be. Almost apathetic. "Just handle it, Miles," became his mantra.

"The same unsub?" he asked before I could say hello.

"Probably."

"And?"

"This second murder most likely takes Frank Sinclair out of the equation. Unless he did it to camouflage the first, which I doubt. So, this brings us back to square one."

"Keep at it. You'll get him."

"I intend to."

"Be careful, Miles."

"I beg your pardon?"

"I hear the vultures are out, looking for blood," the sheriff said ominously.

"Those two again?" I shook my head.

"Yes, I'm afraid so. Where are you now?"

"About two minutes from my office."

"Well—be prepared for a shit-storm."

The line went dead.

* * *

It was now close to 10:00 p.m. I walked into my office knowing exactly who'd be there waiting for me. "Vultures" was the sheriff's and my codeword for the mayors of Bonita Springs and Fort Myers, who were right now making themselves at home. The former was a bear of a man, nine years my junior but weighing quite a bit more. The latter was closer to me in age and size.

Both were dressed formally in suits and ties. Bruce Hillier of Bonita Springs was seated in the chair behind my desk. Middle-aged, the man's complexion was always beet red. I suspected a blood pressure issue. Leo Torbram stood on his right next to the desk and in close proximity.

In theory I reported to Sheriff Norman, but the mayor of Bonita Springs not only had a vested interest, he was ultimately responsible for my position. No matter the circumstance, however, I didn't appreciate his unannounced visit, and I especially disliked him occupying my chair.

"What can I do for you?" I asked, implying my displeasure.

"There's been another murder," Hillier said, his tone of voice accusatory, like it was my fault.

Duhhh, I wanted to say.

"That's two murders in less than two weeks."

"And?"

"And?" His lips formed a tight slash. "I'd like to know what you're doing about it. Bonita Springs doesn't have murders. We're one of the safest communities in all of Florida. Perhaps in all of the United States. If word leaks out, our property values will plummet."

"I see."

"We need to know what progress is being made," Leo Torbram piped up. "Are there any suspects? Whom have you interviewed? What steps are being taken to prevent a *third* occurrence?"

What steps, my ass. How many times had I explained to these clowns what my job entailed? I should be getting on with my investigation, not standing here, wasting my breath. "I can assure you," I said, using a tired cliché, "that everything that should be done is being done. My people are working around the clock. But this'll take time. Barring a miracle, probably ten more days."

"Ten more days!" both men exclaimed at once.

"That's right. If we're lucky. Mrs. Sinclair ordered a pizza on the night she was murdered. We had to track down the deliveryman, be sure his alibi was solid and rule him out. Then we had to interview Frank Sinclair's fishing buddies, be sure they corroborated his story. Based on their reputation, while they were likely doing more screwing around than fishing, they were still together at the time of Cathy Sinclair's murder. We've also been interviewing the service contractors: pool technicians, plumbers, electricians, carpenters, bug control people, and handymen. The list is endless…"

"Ten more days, and then what?" Mayor Hillier demanded.

"If no suspects turn up, we'll move on to the residents themselves. There are twenty-two hundred homes on site. Nearly four thousand people in all. No matter how you look at it, it's a formidable task."

"And how long will that take? Ten additional days?"

"Or longer."

The man's red face colored even more. "Well, you don't have that goddamn luxury. You either come up with a shorter timeframe, or you'll find yourself in jeopardy."

I almost burst out laughing. "In jeopardy for doing my job?"

"That's correct," Mayor Torbram interrupted. "Isn't that what Bruce just said?"

I turned toward him. "He did, but I wanted it clarified. Look, I'm sorry, gentlemen, but if you have a problem with my performance, you should take it up with my immediate supervisor—Sheriff Norman."

Mayor Hillier came out of my chair in a fury, his breathing sounding impaired. "Enough!" he hollered. "I think it would be best if you recused yourself from this case!"

Recused? What am I—a lawyer? I mused.

"Or better still, hand in your resignation."

"My resignation?"

"That's right. You know what they say—if you can't stand the heat in the kitchen, get out."

I know what's going on here. Hank Broderick, the ex-deputy sheriff of Lee County—a crony of Mayor Hillier's—had recently resurfaced. Hillier was angling to get his friend back in my job.

I took my time, moving the opposite way around the desk to sit in my chair.

"So, what's it going to be?" Hillier glared at me.

"What will be will be," I taunted. "Now—get the hell out of my office … gentlemen."

Mayor Hillier did his best to save face. "As of now, you're on the clock. If you don't have a suspect in custody within two weeks, we'll instruct the sheriff to demand your resignation."

I'd said my piece and was done talking. Head down, I shuffled through some paperwork, ignoring them. Without another word, they filed out of my office. I resolved that I'd risk being fired before I'd kiss any mayoral ass.

9

20+ years ago

My father was a first-generation policeman in Phoenix, Arizona. I never wanted to be anything but a cop myself and naturally followed in his footsteps.

At the age of twenty-five I married my twenty-three-year-old girlfriend, Alice Knox, a petite brunette with green eyes. Alice was a secretary in a law office. We each kept long hours and both enjoyed what we did.

A few years later an opportunity for advancement presented itself with the Chicago Police Department. I was reluctant to accept the offer as it'd mean leaving the only city either of us had known. I decided to delay my answer.

Three weeks became a month. Chicago grew impatient. I talked it over with Alice and she encouraged me: Not accepting the job would lead to second guessing myself later in life. Did I want to look back when it was too late and feel regret? The time for career advancement was now, she insisted, while I was still young.

I suspected she was saying these things strictly for my benefit, but her words were convincing. I called Chicago and negotiated the terms of my employment.

Like any move of this nature there was a learning curve; finding my way around a new city, getting used to severe winter weather. It was fortunate I had Alice by my side. Every complaint I made was countered by sage advice.

We settled into a routine. Alice found a job with a legal firm close to home. And, unusual for Chicago, I didn't have more than a half-hour drive to work. Starting a family became our next priority.

We did away with prophylactics and took to experimenting with new and challenging positions. It brought both of us heightened pleasure, yet nothing worked. Alice couldn't conceive, no matter what we tried. We spent too many hours discussing it, stressing over it, wondering if it wasn't meant to be.

We talked about adoption. Alice was in favor; I was not. It became a moot point four months later when her gynecologist confirmed her pregnancy. But Alice didn't have an easy time of it; morning sickness lasted forever.

By the time she was admitted to the hospital we already knew it was a boy. Contractions were timed; anxiety gave way to pain and seven hours later Charles was born. Alice was too exhausted to rejoice, but I was fueled by relief. I went on a cigar passing binge to doctors and nurses, interns, and even total strangers.

Charles wasn't a happy baby. While not colic, the symptoms he displayed were of a similar nature. When he wasn't crying, he was coughing. Instead of smiling, he was whining.

Our lives were no longer normal. Sleep for Alice and me became erratic. Charles had to be constantly monitored. I consulted our pediatrician so often I was making a nuisance of myself.

We discussed a live-in nanny. It would be a squeeze financially but well worth it. We hired a woman from England. Elizabeth Crane began with us on a Monday. On the following Saturday, she quit. Even a seasoned professional couldn't handle our cantankerous child.

* * *

At the age of two, Charles was into violent temper tantrums. If he didn't get his way, he'd throw whatever happened to be within reach. It could be his dinner plate, the cutlery, or his glass. Anything not tied down or too heavy was at risk. Alice and I often bore the brunt of his projectiles. As did the nannies, when they were still with us. Three more had already been hired and bailed.

We desperately wanted to believe neither of us was at fault. Until now we'd seldom argued, rarely picked on one another, never cast blame; but the strain was starting to show.

At the age of four my son's moods were getting worse. He'd mope around the house or explode with fits of temper.

At six Charles was sent home for talking back to his teacher. We reprimanded our son by confining him to his room. There would be no television, no video games. Instead of teaching him a lesson it fueled his anger even more. He busted up every toy that was breakable; and the ones that weren't he flung out the window.

We engaged a child psychologist and Charles began bi-weekly sessions. Progress was slow in coming. I thought it was nonexistent. Alice—the eternal optimist—claimed she could see a glimmer of hope.

When our son turned ten, he was accused of cheating on an exam. We were called in for a meeting with his teacher and a guidance counselor. My wife and I became less civil with each other; I blamed her, she blamed me.

In Charles' fifteenth year, Alice noticed the odd piece of jewelry would go missing. As a test she purposely left an old cubic zirconia ring of hers on the bedroom dresser in plain sight. She told Charles she was going out for a couple of hours. Upon her return the ring was gone.

My police instincts urged me to take action; I didn't know any other way. I wanted to interrogate our son until the truth came out. However, my wife counseled restraint, and I obeyed her wishes.

Charles' first arrest—for the robbery of a gas-bar attendant—came at age seventeen; and I could tell Alice couldn't take anymore. She quit her job and simply lost interest. There was no inertia, no get-up-and-go. Instead of discussing our son's situation she argued with me. I often noticed her words slurring. She became irritable and could barely hold a thought or carry on a meaningful conversation.

I suspected the cause. It didn't take long to discover a stash of prescription drugs carelessly hidden in her bathroom. Our arguments grew more frequent and more intense. I began to stay away, preferring liquid dinners in bars to the alternative.

Charles stint at university lasted one semester. His entry into the workforce was no better. He failed at whatever job he tried; car-wash attendant, busboy in a restaurant, burger flipper at McDonald's. The chip on his shoulder never failed to alienate his employers.

And his friends were of no help. A motley crew of angry

blacks, trailer-trash whites and knife-carrying Hispanics. Not a congenial one in the bunch; quick tempered and prone to violence, menacing in their manner, eager to challenge authority.

The more often Charles brought them home, the more nervous and agitated Alice became. She stood by, helpless, as our son and his buddies locked themselves in his room and played heavy metal rock at ear-splitting decibels.

I learned the truth in one of my wife's few lucid moments and I took action. I searched Charles' room and found a stash of cocaine and amphetamines. When I confronted him, my son swore he wasn't a user himself, just a dealer, as if that made a difference. I warned him to change his ways or I'd have no choice but to have him arrested.

The hatred in my son's eyes intensified.

* * *

I took to imbibing during the day. I kept a flask in my desk at work as well as one in my car. Breath mints were my constant companion. If I arrived home at a decent hour Alice would pick a fight. If I arrived home late, I'd find her passed out on the couch.

My "woe is me" attitude grew worse and constantly sought blame. Charles was culpable because of the way he turned out; my wife was at fault because she'd turned to drugs.

Guy Thomas, the captain at my precinct, warned me to ease up on booze or face suspension. I was stunned. Until that moment I had no idea that he or anyone else knew about my drinking problem.

After Alice and I were married I'd often dream of having a son to bond with. Instead of basking in the father/son relationship

I'd visualized, I was burdened with a boy possessed with an attitude so foreign to me, I couldn't understand it, let alone cope.

When Alice told me she was afraid of Charles, of what he was liable to do, I considered telling him to move out. After all, he was twenty-one; time he made it on his own. But our son had no means of support. Even if I paid his rent, how would Charles manage the rest of his life? Out of our sight he'd soon become even more of a liability.

My wife's complaints became more frantic. Charles had taken to threatening her, she said, demanding money, food for his friends, or the use of her car. I began questioning my ability to be a husband as well as a father. The more I admitted my own failure the more I drank.

Alice lost a lot of weight and grew sloppy. She'd often remain in bed all day. And I took the easy way out. My drinking escalated. I no longer had a sense of obligation; my mind could barely focus.

I got the call at eleven o'clock in the morning. I was at work. A woman's voice I could hardly recognize muttered, "C-Come h-home."

"Huh?"

"P-Please ... h-home."

"Alice?"

No response.

"Alice! Tell me what's wrong!"

"I ... I shot him, Miles. I ... shot Charles ... with your gun."

10

January 21

Denise Gerigk said goodbye to the other women and walked out of Jill Derbyshire's house. As usual she was dressed stylishly; pink flowered top and red- Bermuda shorts, blonde hair combed to perfection, makeup applied with care. Nine-thirty at night and her mid-week bridge game had just ended.

She got in her Audi A4 and started the motor. The drive home would take twelve minutes or less. The night was beautiful and she could see multiple star formations in the sky.

About to enter her neighborhood of Augusta, the car sputtered; Denise hardly had enough time to guide it to the curb when it died. The control panel remained lit. She quickly glanced at the fuel gauge: EMPTY.

Not again! she thought. *What's this? The second time in less than two months?*

There was no one to blame but herself. Of late she'd gotten into the habit of putting off the onerous task of filling her gas tank ... until the inevitable happened.

She stepped out, locked the Audi and leaned against it. Her husband was home watching one of the rare Toronto Maple Leaf hockey games being shown on Florida television. Disturbing him and asking for a lift would only make her feel more foolish. Calling one of the women she'd just played cards with would be equally belittling.

It's a nice night. I'll walk, she decided. Her hand automatically patted her Coach bag for reassurance. Inside was a compact 9mm Beretta just like the ones her girlfriends were also carrying wherever they went. Once she'd completed the brief but thorough training course, Denise had become comfortable with the gun. By her estimation there were four more blocks to go. *What can happen in four blocks?*

* * *

Born in Montreal to French Canadian parents, Denise Bernier spoke little English while growing up. Her father died at the age of forty-nine when she was thirteen. There was no insurance and not very much in the way of savings. Denise thought of that period of her life as the "dark side" because of the mess she'd gotten into; a situation that to this day remained unspoken about.

She had a brother and two sisters. They all pitched in to make ends meet. More than a full year passed before Denise came out of her funk. She began to work when class let out and on weekends at whatever temporary jobs she could find. After graduating high school she took a full-time position as a teller at a local branch of the Bank of Montreal.

Promotion followed promotion. By the age of twenty-one her English had vastly improved and she was transferred to the main downtown branch. Tom Gerigk, a salesman for the Hasbro toy company in Canada, eleven years her senior and married, was a regular customer.

The two became friendly. Two years later, when his marriage came undone, Tom asked her out. Denise had recently been dumped by her Anglophone boyfriend who reneged on his promise to always be there for her. She liked Tom, and it wasn't only his mesmerizing blue eyes. Despite the typical salesman's bluster, there was something about him; a kind demeanor and a gentle soul.

Tom left Hasbro and started his own toy distribution company. When he moved to Toronto, Denise figured she'd never see him again. But then came his surprising invitation for her to join him; and her delighted acceptance. Within weeks they were living and working together. Marriage soon followed.

The toy industry proved to be a challenge. But Denise loved what she did; discovering she was a kid at heart. However, her adapted business was a crapshoot. The key retailers like MyMart and Arrow were becoming more difficult to deal with. Promised purchase orders from these and other large chains sometimes failed to materialize, thereby leaving them with excess inventory and storage costs.

Still, Tom proved to be frugal, and they were able to save enough to buy their home in Florida. It was a dream come true for both of them; having a warm-weather place where they could relax during the winter months. Though invariably, Denise would use it more often than Tom, as business matters in Canada occupied his time more than hers.

She made friends with many of her American neighbors and it was an eye opener. She'd come to the conclusion that Canadians as a whole were more conservative, laidback, and accommodating. A disproportionate number of Americans were opinionated, too serious about their politics, and far more prejudiced.

*   *   *

Almost home, Denise was passing Randal Park, named for one of the founders of Bonita Palms. Seventy-five square yards, with a goldfish pond in the center, benches, and few trees or thick foliage that someone could hide behind. Denise and Tom spent many Sundays here, kicking back and enjoying the sun.

Denise abruptly came up short. A pebble had become stuck in her left Cole Haan shoe. She thought about toughing it out, but it was really bothering her. She hobbled on the crushed gravel path toward the nearest bench.

She was about to take a seat when she lurched back awkwardly in alarm. Millipedes. Dozens of them. Slithering on the ground close to the bench. She despised the wormy creatures. The fact that they were harmless did nothing to ease her anxiety. They appeared when you least expected, but not usually this early in the year, especially not in January.

She limped to the next bench over, made sure it was clear of the insect infestation, and took a seat, setting her bag beside her. Then she froze. The sudden movement when she'd first spotted the millipedes must have reactivated the twitch in the right side of her neck. Actually, more than a twitch; the damn pain seemed to travel from head to toe.

Denise couldn't count the number of doctors she'd consulted, both here in Florida and back home in Toronto. General practitioners. Physiotherapists. Chiropractors. Each had come up with a different diagnosis. One specialist told her it was N.U.C.A. or cervical artery dissection. Another blamed it on the Atlas bone at the bottom of her cranium. A third mentioned entrapped nerves which, from her understanding, was like a grouping of neurons being pinched together.

When painkiller pills and muscle relaxants failed Denise, her doctor theorized there could be a psychological trigger, such as anxiety, and prescribed Narvia. She reached into her bag where she now kept a travel pack and removed two pills, then used the water bottle she always had with her and washed them down.

Denise bent over and removed her shoe, shook it, and a dime-sized pebble fell out. A high-pitched whine cut through the air, disturbing the quiet. She put her shoe back on and stood up. A helicopter, flying low, was getting closer.

This isn't unusual, she reminded herself. Often there were medical emergencies that required transportation of a Bonita Palms resident to Lee Memorial Hospital in Fort Myers, the closest one with a helipad. The helicopter would land just inside the main gate at the intersection of the two key roads. Denise assumed this was the case now.

The sound grew louder. She was looking up, expecting to see the helicopter zip by at any moment, just as something else caught her eye: someone slowly approaching on foot, along the same path she'd used a few moments ago.

In a panic, she thrust her hand into her bag, pulled out the Beretta and flicked off the safety the way she'd been shown.

She sized up the figure as an African American male. The helicopter was almost directly above her, the noise so loud it hurt her ears. Her attention flipped between the copter and the man. She raised the gun to waist level.

The helicopter was moving slowly. Denise called out as loudly as she could to be heard above the din, "WHO ... ARE ... YOU?"

The person didn't answer.

"I have a gun."

His pace continued.

"SIR?!"

Denise didn't know what to do. *Can he not hear me? Or is he deliberately disobeying me?* A voice in her head commanded, *Shoot! Shoot now and ask questions later!*

The man drew nearer.

Noise from the helicopter began fading into the distance.

"HOLD IT!" Denise screamed, "RIGHT THERE!" her knees knocking together. She raised the gun to shoulder level, her finger tightening on the trigger, when the pain in her neck flared again.

"Mrs. Gerigk?"

That the man knew her name stunned her. "Y-Yes?"

"It's Martin ... Martin Williams," he said, arms outstretched in a defensive manner.

Martin Williams? The boy was eighteen years old and lived with his parents in Augusta part-time when he wasn't attending college. He performed chores for her and her husband as well as others in the neighborhood. Martin was one of the most reliable people she'd ever met. "Oh my God!" An involuntary sound of relief, almost a giggle, escaped her lips. "Martin ... Williams..."

"Yes, it's me." He'd stopped in his tracks, his gaze switching from Denise's face to the gun she was pointing at his chest.

Embarrassment washed over her. She flicked the safety back on and shoved the gun into her bag. Denise massaged the tension in her neck while explaining about her car; then being disturbed by the loud helicopter as, what she believed to be a complete stranger, was advancing on her. "W-What are you doing out here?" she asked.

"I just got back into town. A friend left me off at the main gate. I was walking home when I saw you—thought you might need some help."

She shuddered. "I'm so sorry. I..."

It finally dawned on Martin. "Of course..." now Martin was embarrassed, "of course you'd be frightened, being approached in the dark—by *anyone*." He pointed in the direction of her house. "Would you like me to walk you home?"

She forced a smile. "I'm fine now, Martin. Thanks for your concern."

* * *

During the remaining two blocks to her house, Denise couldn't stop berating herself. She'd come this close to shooting an innocent boy. She was ashamed of the voice in her head, ordering her, *Shoot now ... ask questions later.* Would she have had the same thought if the person had been white? What about her theory that Canadians were less prejudiced than Americans?

She was trembling as she climbed the short steps to her front door.

Twenty-nine hundred square feet. A cathedral ceiling. Four bedrooms, two full baths, and a decent-sized pool. Denise took pride in every inch of it.

Tom heard her enter, turned off the TV, and approached. "Did you win?" he asked.

Without a word, she collapsed in his arms and broke into tears.

"Denise?"

She couldn't speak; wished she could nest where she was for a good long time.

"Honey—what is it?"

It all came out in a rush: Her car running out of gas so deciding to walk, the helicopter and Martin Williams, the gun she'd removed from her bag, the voice in her head telling her to use it.

"You walked?" Her husband was stunned. "You should have called me! I would've come get you!"

"I ... didn't want to disturb your hockey game."

"Who cares about the damn game? Two women have been murdered, Denise."

The fact that he was this concerned about her welfare touched her heart. "Okay, okay, I get it," she said. "Yes, I should've called you."

His voice softened. "Did you really come that close to shooting the boy?"

"I did..."

Tom proffered a handkerchief.

She took it from him. They were standing in the brightly-lit foyer. Denise faced a mirror that lined the opposite wall. She caught her own reflection, then Tom's. And she paused.

There was a quarter-full glass of scotch sitting on the side table. Her husband liked to drink but seldom after dinner. And there was more. Something in his disposition. She'd been so self-absorbed she hadn't noticed it when she first entered the house.

"C'mon. Let's have a seat," Tom said, indicating the off-white leather couch in the great room.

As he led the way, Denise's eyes lit on the two-foot

polished-bronze statue of Jesus, positioned on a pedestal next to the couch. She'd purchased the statue while on a vacation in Rome. Something about the pose—Jesus welcoming the children onto Him—had appealed to her. She paused, crossed herself and whispered a Hail Mary.

Tom gave her a funny look. This was the first time in ages she'd said or done anything devotional. "What's wrong?"

"No," she didn't hesitate, "what's wrong with *you* is the question."

"What do you mean?"

"Tom?"

"What?"

"Dis moi."

"It's ... nothing."

"Please?" she insisted.

"Let's talk about what happened to you."

She turned so she was facing him. She saw how drained he looked. Tom was a youthful sixty-nine. People often mistook him to be much younger. But not tonight. She could see the stress on his face. And she had a pretty good hunch what was causing it. The toy industry in Canada was getting worse. Buyers were practically teenagers without experience, gutless merchandise managers, and a retail environment run by bean-counters.

"Can I get you a drink?" Tom offered.

"No." Her concern ramped up. "Tom ... tell me."

"You don't want to know," he sighed.

She went to stand from the couch; the pain radiated again. *Not now!* she berated herself.

"Your neck?"

She tried to nod; couldn't quite manage it. "I wanted to get you your drink."

"In your condition? You sit. I'll get it." He came to his feet, retrieved his glass and returned to the couch. He took a long sip, then said, "You know how we've been saying that Arrow's arrogance is going to hurt them one day?"

It was a sore topic. Instead of buying the Leaders chain when the American dollar was valued thirty percent higher than the Canadian dollar, Arrow hesitated until it was at par, then vastly overpaid. And unlike MyMart's entry into Canada, where small steps were taken to enable success, Arrow chose to open all 130+ stores nearly at once, before they had a decent logistics system in place. Store shelves were never more than half-filled from the get-go. Pricing of goods was higher than most if not all of Arrow's competitors. Management talked itself into believing that they were perfectly knowledgeable about the retail environment in Canada. Hiring executives with Canadian experience was unnecessary. The Arrow name alone would be enough to guarantee success.

Goose bumps erupted on Denise's skin. "What about them?"

"You'll find this hard to believe."

"Tell me."

"They've just declared bankruptcy."

She looked at Tom askance. Many had predicted it would only be a matter of time, but not this soon. "Why are they giving up after less than two years? It doesn't make sense."

Tom muttered something under his breath. Instead of asking him to repeat himself, Denise allowed the seconds to tick by, an inevitable question on the tip of her tongue.

Her husband read her mind: "$976,000."

She reeled back in disbelief. "That's what they owe us?"

"'Fraid so."

"But Arrow Canada is a wholly-owned subsidiary of Arrow U.S. The parent company isn't going bankrupt. They're still a viable concern. Surely to God the Canadian government has regulations in place that protect us." She paused, then asked weakly, *"N'est-ce pas?"*

"Uh-uh. I'm afraid not."

Denise knew their operating line at the bank was supported by second mortgages on both the house in Toronto and the one here in Florida. They'd also loaned their business $500,000. A loss of this magnitude would ruin them.

Tom tried to reassure her. "It isn't the end of the world. We've been through tough times before. Look at me—"

She tried to turn her head; felt her neck resist.

He gently placed both hands on her shoulders. "Denise—we can do it again. I … need you to be strong."

She couldn't find her voice. She and Tom lived life to its fullest. And yes, they'd built a modest nest egg. But their retirement depended on one day selling the business and getting out from their guarantees to the bank. Without that, both homes would have to go. She remembered growing up poor; the thought of returning to that kind of existence sent chills up her spine.

11

20+ years ago

"*I shot him with your gun.*"

The words rang in my ears like a point-blank explosion. The gun my wife was referring to was the legal spare I kept locked in the top desk drawer in my home office. I had no idea she was aware of its existence, or how she knew where to find the key to the drawer.

I dashed out of my office, mind in turmoil, and drove like a madman, lights flashing, siren blaring, causing anything in my way—be they cars or pedestrians—to scamper for safety.

I made it home in record time and screeched to a stop, half on the lawn. I jumped out of the car, motor left running, and blew through the front door.

My wife stood inside the vestibule. She was wearing an old, worn-out nightgown. Her eyes were spooked. She was holding my .38 in her hand.

"Alice?"

She turned toward me without speaking.

I ran to her, praying I'd somehow misinterpreted what I'd heard on the phone, that this was all a mistake.

But Charles was lying facedown on the hardwood floor in the hallway just outside his bedroom, a great amount of blood pooled beneath his upper body. His legs were splayed out and both arms were flat; his switchblade near the curved fingers of his right hand.

I dropped to my knees and placed my hand on my son's carotid artery, needing to double check what I was already sure about.

My wife stood opposite, shaking as if about to have a seizure. "Is he…"

I got to my feet and silently nodded yes. I carefully took the gun she was still holding out of her hand and eased it into my pocket.

She described what had happened, veering in and out of hysteria: Charles demanded money. She refused to give in this time. He slapped her in the face and headed for his bedroom. "I … instinctively knew he was going for his knife," she said. "He's done it before … threatened to cut me if I didn't give him what he wanted."

My wife's voice dropped; I had to strain to hear her. She'd known for years about my spare gun and where to find the key. She hurried to my office, got the key taped beneath the center desk drawer, took out the gun … "to protect myself. Charles came out of his bedroom with the knife, high on something and acting crazy, slashing the knife through the air. I … thought he was going to kill me. I pleaded with him to stop. I *begged* him. But he lunged at me … and I shot him. It happened so fast I didn't have time to think."

I wrapped Alice in my arms. The frailness of her body surprised me. I could only imagine how much weight she'd lost.

A solution played out in my mind. I knew what I had to do. My actions in the next few minutes would determine her fate. I guided my wife into the master bathroom, lowered the lid on the toilet and helped her take a seat. I carefully cleaned her hands with a washcloth until I was sure no gunshot residue remained. I then took the gun out of my pocket and had her grip it to reset her fingerprints.

"We need a story," I slowly explained. "You called me at work in a panic. Charles was hopped up on cocaine and acting crazy. You begged me to come home. I left the office in a hurry and drove like a bat out of hell. Inside the house I found Charles holding you in a chokehold with one hand, brandishing his knife with the other. My spare gun was lying by your feet. You had taken it out but couldn't bring yourself to use it, so you dropped it. I picked up the gun and told Charles to let you go. He released you then lunged at me. We struggled and the gun accidentally went off. "

I paused.

"Alice?"

She remained mum.

"Do you understand what I said?"

Her nod was slight but perceptible.

"This is imperative, Alice. We need to tell the police it was *me* who shot our son."

* * *

I helped my wife into bed, then went back to the bathroom where I'd left the gun. I felt emotionally spent and had to pull myself together. I hurried down to the basement and fired a bullet into the wall to add the necessary residue to my hand, providing evidence that I was the one who shot it, corroborating my story.

Back upstairs I kept my mind blank as I passed by my son's body and dropped the gun next to him.

I returned to the bedroom. My wife was lying on her back, her breathing shallow, eyes open but unfocussed.

I spoke her name.

She didn't move.

"Alice—please. Listen to me. I have to call the police. Too much time's already passed. I need to know you've got our story straight."

Not getting a response, I nudged her shoulder.

She turned her head toward me and blinked.

"Do you know what we have to tell the police?" I pressed.

"I ... know," she acknowledged.

* * *

I was instructed to take a paid leave of absence. Quitting booze cold turkey played havoc with my body. It got so bad I had to check myself into rehab. Luckily, a neighbor promised to look in on Alice.

I went through the roughest patch of my life. Severe nausea accompanied by tremors I thought would never end. By the time I came out I saw things in a clearer light. My withdrawal pains gave way to mental anguish. How does anyone overcome the loss of a child ... no matter how troubled that child may have been?

I was to blame for what my wife had done. It was her finger on the trigger, yet I was the one responsible. Time and again she'd warned me about Charles' behavior. Rather than act I'd escaped; at Alice's peril, it turned out.

The investigation took months. In between there were numerous meetings with our lawyer, Tim Walsh. It was one thing to lie, quite another to have others believe it. I didn't know if we were being successful or not.

My wife and I were interviewed separately and together. The specialists had all been called. By the time Walsh reached us by phone to give us the verdict, I was a nervous wreak.

"Justifiable homicide," he said, baritone voice booming in my ear.

"For real?"

"For real. Your testimony was compelling. Your son's friends helped by admitting Charles was losing control. The authorities are closing their case without pressing charges."

My relief was palpable.

"You still there?"

I cleared my throat. "Tim … I can't thank you enough."

After disconnecting I turned to Alice. "It's over. We can get on with our lives. I've been exonerated."

At first, there was no reaction. "Exonerated?" my wife muttered dully.

"Yes … declared innocent." I grabbed her shoulders, wanting to celebrate, to make this a new beginning.

Alice edged away from me. "I'm tired. I think I'll go lie down."

* * *

The following morning, she took her first shower in weeks. I waited for the water to shut off before going to see her. Alice was still toweling off and I drew in my breath.

Her breasts had shrunk to emaciated orbs. Her arms looked frail. And her legs, once her best feature, were now feeble sticks of sagging skin.

Alice put on her nightgown and took a seat in front of the mirror.

I approached and asked if I could brush her hair.

She nodded.

It'd been many months since we'd been intimate; this felt as intimate as it was going to get.

Less than a minute passed when my wife turned to me and said, in words fraught with pain, "I murdered our son."

* * *

I went back to work, came home most days for lunch, arrived early for dinner. I told myself Alice was marginally improving. But her zoned-out state concerned me more and more.

I took to washing whatever pills of hers I found down the toilet. Crespon, and one called Melocontine, which I was sure was an opioid. My wife would invariably come up with a new supply of one or more. I reasoned with her: "You need help. I'll find a therapist. Someone you can talk to."

She neither consented nor protested.

Appointment after appointment was made but each was canceled. She kept coming up with one excuse after another.

* * *

I planned an intervention. If Alice refused to see a therapist, I'd have one come to her. Before I could make the arrangements, however, I came home from work on a Wednesday evening and was surprised to find my wife dressed and wearing makeup. The blouse and slacks she wore swam on her. But at least she'd forsaken her nightgown.

I stood in the vestibule, mute.

"I made dinner," she said.

I washed up and took a seat in the dining room. For the first time in ages, Alice had lit the candles. I watched her approach the stove. She returned carrying a plate filled with what could have been fish or chicken. The top layer had been burned so badly I couldn't tell for sure.

Yet, I didn't complain. I tried my first forkful. It was chicken and it was tough. But it tasted like the most wonderful meal of my life. We didn't say much to each other. Once dinner was over, I cleared the table and Alice handled the dishes.

"Thank you," I said.

She didn't reply but I was more encouraged than I'd been in months.

* * *

The next morning I left the house before six and was forced to skip lunch. I was working on a new case that required my full attention. The day flew by and I arrived home exhausted. The lights were off and the blinds were drawn.

"Alice?" I called and walked into the bedroom.

She was naked, lying on top of the sheets, unconscious. The

hair on the back of my neck bristled. I threw a blanket over Alice, swooped her up in my arms and made a dash for the door.

I positioned her as gently as I could manage in the back seat of my car. I talked to her as I drove, hoping beyond hope that she'd respond; knowing she wouldn't, but trying nevertheless.

The hospital was normally a twenty-minute drive. A light snow was falling and the roads were slippery. I still made it in fifteen minutes flat. I parked in front, rushed to the door, and called for help. An orderly and an intern hurried out. I could do nothing but watch while Alice was transported on a gurney.

The waiting room was jammed with every seat taken. I stood in a corner and tried to divert my thoughts.

"Mr. Delany?"

I nearly vaulted forward.

A young doctor with brown hair and dark eyes approached. He looked worn out. "Your wife is comatose," he said matter-of-factly. "We pumped her stomach. Tried everything to revive her. I'm not sure she'll survive the night. You might want to notify the rest of her family."

I thought of lashing out at his indifference, then reconsidered. "Yes. Well. I'm the only one."

* * *

Memories haunted me: Alice and I first starting to date. Graduating university. Getting married. The way she eased the transition when we moved from Phoenix to Chicago. Trying to have a baby. Her joyous reaction after she found out she was finally pregnant.

How did it go so wrong? I shook my head. Who was I kidding?

It went wrong because of what I'd done; selfishly not caring; going on a permanent bender; hurting the people who mattered the most.

The night dragged on. The crowd thinned but the room never completely emptied. Every few hours I'd get an update on my wife's condition. Little had changed: Alice was on a respirator to help her breathe. The latest electroencephalogram showed diminished brain activity.

I realized she intended for last night's meal to be her goodbye. Finding her made up and dressed had felt too good to be true. And it *was* too good. I should have known, or at least suspected.

The same doctor approached at six o'clock in the morning, looking even more exhausted. "I'm sorry, Mr. Delany," he said, finally with a little empathy, "but we need a decision about removing life support."

"Now?"

"Yes. I'm afraid so. Would you come with me, please?"

I followed him into an isolated cubical. A half dozen machines were monitoring Alice's vital signs, each making a sound I detested.

The doctor pointed out the one that read her brain waves. The ripple in the line was barely perceptible. "Do we have your permission?"

I turned my attention to the bed. My wife wasn't merely pale, she was ghost-like. Her face had shrunk into itself. I touched her cheek, found it frigid. I kissed the spot I'd touched.

"Mr. Delany?"

I reluctantly turned. The doctor was proffering a document and pen. I snatched both from his hand. "I'd like some privacy."

"Of course," he acknowledged and left.

* * *

The feeding tube, breathing apparatus, and other devices were removed. I was told my wife wasn't suffering, but I didn't believe it. Three days later she died.

I racked my brain for a time afterwards. I was of two minds as to why I took the blame for my son's death. Was it, as I wanted to believe, to protect Alice from the strain of an intensive investigation and possibly being prosecuted? Or was I worried that her claim of acting in self-defense was suspect?

I handed in my resignation and put the house up for sale. There was constant chatter in my head, reminding me of my culpability in Alice's death. I doubted I'd ever find inner peace again.

On occasion I'd drive by a liquor store and slow down. Something always prevented me from coming to a full stop. I felt I owed it to the memory of my wife and son to walk the path of sobriety for the rest of my life.

* * *

After burying Charles and Alice I left Chicago and ended up in my hometown of Phoenix for a while, where almost everything was different from what I remembered. Old friends, for the most part, weren't as friendly; old haunts not as familiar. Even renewing family ties was a challenge; they didn't make me feel welcome at all.

I decided to travel across the U.S. My car was a rusted-out Chevy Impala with over 100,000 miles on it and tires so worn I could see the steel belts. I wondered which would give out first—the tires or the motor. I vowed to keep going until one or the other quit on me.

My stubborn self-incrimination never left; whether during the day while driving, or at night while having take-out dinner or watching television in a cheap motel room. Sleep was a constant challenge. I couldn't get the death-pallor images of my son and wife out of my head.

I went north to Denver, then east to Minneapolis, Detroit, New York, and Boston; then south from there, with extra time spent in Washington, D.C. By the time I reached the northern tip of Florida my car engine lost the battle, sending a plume of smoke out from under the hood in a final death throe.

I got hold of Guy Thomas, my superior at Chicago PD, which led to an introduction to Sheriff Norman. Two days later I was in Bonita Springs—having traveled by train—being interviewed.

I was told an opening was forthcoming, but I'd have to be patient. The current deputy sheriff, Hank Broderick, was apparently looking to take on a better-paying position in Tampa. Little did I know that later on our paths would cross, and not in a pleasant way.

12

January 23

By noon I needed a reprieve. I'd been tied up in our interview room all morning. Dozens of service people, in and out like a revolving door, yet only two remotely viable suspects: Turk Lagerfeld, a 30-year-old technician with Comcast whose story changed twice; and Harold Brown, a 47-year-old electrician with Florida Power and Light who'd lied about where he was when the first murder was committed.

I was grasping at anything I could find. Eight years in the sheriff's department and I'd never encountered a conundrum like the one I was facing now; a killer with no clear motive.

Meanwhile, I assigned Pedersen and Wellington to the task of interviewing friends and relatives of the deceased women, hoping one of them could offer us a lead. But I kept Barbara Miller for myself, on a strong hunch she knew a lot more about Frank Sinclair than she was saying.

Traffic was unusually light. I had called Mrs. Miller to ask if I could talk to her about the case, and she'd readily agreed. We were familiar with one another, of course, having met again as recently as a week ago at Cathy Sinclair's memorial.

Barbara greeted me with an effusive smile, in a diaphanous yellow blouse and a black skirt that barely reached a third of the way to her knees. Her dark hair was piled high and held in place by a rhinestone-studded comb.

"Bill's still out, so you're stuck with lil' ole me," she said with a twinkle in her eye.

Presently, Bill was being waylaid by Pedersen, at what I knew was his favorite cafe. I'd planned the interview with Barbara accordingly, figuring she wouldn't talk about Frank with Bill in the room.

She led the way to the couch in the great room. "Can I get you something?"

It sounded like there was more to her invitation. Mrs. Miller was not only attractive, she had an aura of overt sexuality that could make any man feel uncomfortable.

"No, this won't take long," I promised.

"So you said on the phone." Her eyebrow raised slightly. "What would you like to know?"

"I was wondering if you've given the murders any thought? Questioned what the women were doing on the day each died? Considered who might've wanted to do them harm?"

"Considered it? That's all my friends and I have been doing. Going over and over it. It just doesn't make sense."

"What about the husbands?" I asked, getting to the key question. "Especially Frank Sinclair?"

"*Frank?*" she frowned, taken aback. "He had nothing to do with the murders."

"Oh? What makes you so sure?"

"I know him well," she said evenly. "We're friends. Have been for a long while."

Intimate friends? I wanted to ask, but held my tongue.

"When you get to know a person, Sheriff, you learn a lot about them. Get to understand what they're capable of. Frank can no more be a murderer than me." She shot a mischievous glance my way.

I would not be deterred. "Does Mr. Sinclair have any other lady *friends?*"

Barbara Miller fanned her face with her hand as if it were suddenly sweltering inside. "Uh … isn't that something you should ask him?"

* * *

It was too late to return to my office, so I decided to go home. I no sooner entered my house when the phone rang. I answered it in the bedroom.

"Is this the formidable sheriff who always gets his man?"

I smiled to myself. "Might this be the medical examiner who never lets a crime go unresolved?"

"One and the same," Sara Churchill replied. "How was your day, Sheriff?"

"Lovely. Just lovely." I told her about the unproductive interviews and my visit with Mrs. Miller.

"You sound stressed, Miles."

"Do I now?"

"That and in need of relief. I know just what the doctor ordered. Dinner at my house. Friday at seven. No business. You'll have to park your phone and gun at the door."

"My gun as well?"

"You betcha. Do we have a date, or not?"

I didn't have to think about it. "Book it."

* * *

Changed and washed, I stood in front of the medicine cabinet in the master bathroom. The Narvia container was resting by the sink, the one pill that was supposed to ease my anxiety, despite what it did to my stomach. When asked, my doctor advised me to stick with it, saying my system would eventually get used to it.

I'd been debating to stop taking them for a while, so I hesitated. Doing without could lead to a relapse, a possible return to the alcohol I knew I couldn't handle. Did I want to take that risk?

I guess I did. I replaced the pill in the container and walked out of the bathroom, hoping I hadn't made the wrong decision.

13

January 25

Jill Derbyshire was seated in the clubhouse bar with June Adams, one of the assistant pros at Bonita Palms. It was five o'clock on a Thursday afternoon and they had just completed a round of golf.

Jill was wearing her favorite lime-green Jamie Sadock outfit, which she knew went wonderfully with her red hair.

"One more?" June asked, indicating Jill's empty wineglass.

Jill thought for a moment, said, "What the hell? Why not?"

June was in her thirties; a svelte, attractive woman, with a pixie face and porcelain skin. She placed the order for Jill's drink, and was about to say something, when she was interrupted by a young man from the pro shop.

"I apologize for intruding," he said. "We have a—uh—small emergency that we need you to resolve."

The assistant pro looked up at the guy, then down at the table.

Jill could see the hesitation. June most likely wanted to tell the young man to solve the problem himself; after all, she was off duty. But such was the life of golf pros that their time was seldom their own.

"I'll be right there," June said. She came to her feet and apologized to Jill, promising to return as quickly as possible.

Jill watched her go. She'd enjoyed the game today. And she found it sad to think her membership here at Bonita Palms could be coming to an end. She and her husband, Jack…

She paused.

Thinking about her husband reminded her of the teasing they'd been subjected to by their friends when they were first dating, always connecting their names to the nursery rhyme. It was more than "Jack and Jill going up the hill" or "Jack falling down and Jill tumbling after." It quickly became a sonnet, with Jack and Jill placed in grossly embarrassing positions.

But all that was behind them. Soon after graduating college they were married in a simple ceremony in their hometown of Cleveland, Ohio. Three children followed, a boy and two girls, all grown now with families of their own.

Jack had had a successful career with AT&T, in the HR department. She'd been a stay-at-home mom. They had moved into the Palms over twelve years ago. But recently, one of their major financial investments had gone south. A "failsafe" plan proposed by Bill Miller that was turning into a disaster.

Jill couldn't believe they'd ended up in this position. If they didn't find a solution soon, they'd have to sell their Palms house—perhaps give up the idea of a winter home in Florida altogether.

"I'm sorry—"

Jill looked up.

The same guy from the pro shop was back. "June asked me to

tell you she's going to be longer than expected. She asked if she could buy you another drink."

Jill considered it but realized she'd had enough. "No, I'm done. Please tell June I said thanks for the game."

"I will."

When she arrived home, Jill brought in her driver—the latest model from Ping. Her nametag had come loose, and she intended to replace it with one she'd ordered from Pin High.

Jill got undressed planning to luxuriate in a long bath. Jack was in Dallas attending an AT&T alumni reunion, hence there was no one waiting for dinner. She could take as much time as she liked. She ran the water semi-hot, then added a bubble solution.

By the time she toweled off Jill felt refreshed. She took a seat in front of the mirror but dispensed with makeup. She was just taking the hairbrush in hand when she paused.

What was that?

She listened but didn't hear anything. She began to run the brush through her hair, the strokes so even they could have been timed.

There it is again …Oh, the doorbell. Huh? I'm not expecting anyone. Who can it be?

She put the brush down, stood and slipped on her robe. "Coming," she called on her way to the door.

14

7:00 p.m.

Sara Churchill stood in the doorway wearing a dress that was more crimson than red, accenting her well-endowed figure. Her blonde hair cascaded in waves; gold earrings glistening.

"Something the matter?"

It took me a moment to realize I was staring. "Sorry," I said, handing her a bottle of wine.

She read the label. "Umm. *Pouilly Fuissé*. What's the occasion?"

I shrugged. "Only the best for you."

I noticed a coat rack by the door and made a show of removing my jacket; then waving my cell phone for attention, before placing it in one of the pockets. Next I doffed my shoulder holster and gun, and hung everything up.

Sara laughed uproariously while I did this; then gestured the way.

Her coach home, on the lower level, was located close to Fort Myers Beach, but I figured it was distant enough to be reasonably priced. It was my first visit, so Sara took me on a tour. There were two bedrooms and two full bathrooms, a great room, and a den that had been turned into an office.

"Eighteen hundred square feet," Sara said with a measure of pride.

I was surprised to see how the color white dominated and that it somehow worked, contrasted by the teal bedspread in the master bedroom, blue leather couch, and abstract paintings exhibiting various hues of the rainbow.

"Diet Coke?" Sara asked once we reentered the great room.

"Yes, please."

Watching her leave I reminded myself to not rush things. *Slow and easy.*

She was back in a few minutes. "Here you go, *Sheriff*," she said with a wink and a smile.

I accepted the drink and perceived her voice could stir the least prurient of men.

"Cheers," touching her glass with my own.

"*Skol.*" She tasted her martini.

"Is that your first of the night?"

"A lady never tells."

* * *

The dinner began with a shrimp cocktail. Two sauces, one red and spicy, the other a pleasant variation of tartar, adorned the plate. The bread basket included sourdough and whole wheat buns.

"You realize you're a complete mystery to me," Sara said once we began to eat.

"I am?"

"I know nothing about you. Where you were born. If you were ever married. Had any kids. You know—the dull stuff."

I concentrated on my food. "I can't discuss my personal life."

"Oh?" Sara threw an inquisitive look my way. "Why not?"

"I don't know you well enough."

"Seriously?"

"I mean, not well enough at the moment. The night is young. You'll simply have to be patient."

"For how long?"

A smile was my answer.

A Greek salad was served next. Followed by the main course—blackened Florida black grouper, with asparagus and garlic mashed potatoes.

A few bites in I tried bringing up the murders, but Sara stopped me. "No business," she said. And I clamped my mouth shut. Instead, we talked about living in Florida and how fortunate we both were.

Sara insisted on clearing the dishes by herself. A few minutes later, dishwasher running, she joined me in the great room just as I was leaning my head back on the couch, mellowing out.

"Here you go." She handed over a glass of water and settled next to me with a snifter of cognac for herself.

"Who said I wanted water?" I asked, teasing.

She moved a little closer. "You don't want it, don't drink it."

I liked the perfume she was wearing, was about to tell her so, but Sara placed her glass of cognac on top of the wood coffee table, then repositioned herself close to my chest and said, "Close your eyes."

"Uh-uh. I'll fall asleep."

"So?"

"I've more important things in mind."

"Shh." She placed a finger to my lips.

* * *

I jumped when Sara woke me. It hadn't been restful or sleep at all; more like something in-between, a place where time didn't pass; images flashing of women being butchered while people stood and watched, incapable—unwilling—to help them.

"Time for bed, sleepyhead."

"Huh?"

"Can't have you driving home when you're this tired. I've got everything ready in the spare bedroom. C'mon—" She reached out a hand.

I hesitated. I preferred the master bedroom, not the spare, but I reminded myself that I wasn't going to rush things.

The room was also painted white but again there was enough color to make a contrast. The motif was more masculine, with darker shades for the most part.

Sara said good night and left.

Before coming here tonight I'd doubled up on my Narvia medication. Trying to go without was making my anxiety worse. I figured the extra pill was the lesser of two evils. Exceeding the recommended dosage is generally not advised, but I was quite nervous about my date with Sara and realized I needed to calm down.

A new toothbrush sat on the bathroom counter—still in its original package—and a tube of Sensodyne. I brushed my teeth, undressed, and got into bed, but couldn't sleep. Too many thoughts swirled around in my head. About Sara, naturally, but about the murder investigation as well. Trying to figure out who benefited was the real puzzle. *Both victims were known to the perp. I'm certain of it.*

I must have dozed off… Then a woman's naked body—near perfect—stood next to the bed; a butterfly-shaped birthmark about the size of a quarter, slightly above and to the left of her naval.

When she joined me, fingers then hands caressed; mouths then tongues teased. Take it slow, I was telling myself. I didn't want to be aggressive, but I knew that I was anyway. I was losing control. Something was pushing me in a direction I was unable to resist.

* * *

I jolted awake.

Light was streaming in beneath the window blinds. There was no one lying next to me. Was it a dream? I repositioned myself and moved the covers to the side. I was no longer wearing underwear. I sat up and noticed a stain on the sheets. What kind of dream did I have?

I heard Sara in the kitchen. I got up and used the toilet, washed my hands and face, finger-combed my hair and dressed.

Sara was seated at the table, sipping a coffee. I asked what time it was.

She looked up from the newspaper she was reading. "Almost eight."

Her voice was different somehow. Cold and unfriendly. I waited for an invitation to join her. It never came.

"Interesting birthmark," I said.

She didn't comment.

Small bits of last night pieced together, but nothing I could make sense of. Had my physical behavior been disgusting? What actually happened?

I considered asking her but instinctually knew she wouldn't say. Instead, I went to the coat rack and gathered my things.

Sara didn't budge.

"Thanks for dinner." I reached for the doorknob. "Can I see you next week?"

"Call me," she said, not sounding like she meant it.

15

January 26

Debbie Stafford, in the restroom at Cirella's Restaurant on Hwy 41, was having another panic attack. Her watch was missing. One minute it was on her wrist, the next it was gone. The gold Cartier was worth $45,000. One of her favorites, it had been a gift from her husband for her sixtieth birthday.

When did I see it last? she wondered. She remembered putting it on after her shower this evening. But then what? Had she taken it off for some reason? Where? And when?

She sat in the stall cursing herself. This wouldn't be the first time in recent weeks where something of value had been misplaced. *Damn memory. Sixty-six years old and fading fast.* Actually ... not fading but becoming delusional.

Debbie went back to looking for her watch. She dumped the contents of her purse on the cement floor ... comb, brush, compact, lipstick, wallet, pocket-sized packet of Kleenex and cell phone. The watch wasn't there.

She replaced everything in her purse, came out of the

bathroom stall, and approached the sink. One look in the mirror told her more about herself than she cared to know. A double chin threatening to go triple, her puffed cheeks pushing upwards and nearly obliterating her eyes.

Debbie turned on the water, then glanced self-consciously at her hands. Oversized fingers that she was unable to squeeze together without pain. Letting the cold water run, she soaped slowly and meticulously, then dried off with a paper towel.

She'd give anything to not have to return to the table, especially not before finding her watch.

* * *

Larry Stafford, dressed in beige Bermuda shorts and a white golf shirt with the Bonita Palms logo on the sleeve, sat at the table wondering what was taking his wife so long. The others—Tom and Denise Gerigk, Bill and Barbara Miller—were talking amongst themselves. This left him free to consider Debbie; the thought that she could be suffering from early onset Alzheimer's disease scared him half to death.

He prayed he was wrong. That her mood swings, forgetfulness, and recent preoccupation with religion were just a phase she was going through. Getting help for her was foremost on his mind. But how and where would he find someone she'd be willing to see?

Could I place an ad: WANTED. ONE SHAMAN. TO PERFORM A MIRACLE. That wasn't likely to work. But he had no doubt if left untreated his wife's condition would worsen. He was the one living with her. He could see, firsthand, that Debbie was slowly losing her grip on reality. It was up to him to act before it was too late.

***

Barbara Miller, in a low-cut pink blouse and magenta golf shorts, took another bite, then placed her fork on the plate. Chicken Parmigiana was her favorite dish. Yet she found she was no longer hungry. Frank Sinclair had been on her mind all day. The man had stopped calling. One minute he was confessing his undying lust for her—his *need* for her—the next he was completely out of touch, as if being a widower took away his desire for continuing their extramarital affair.

Well, too bad for him, Barbara told herself, absentmindedly glancing in her husband's direction, seated next to her.

Bill was hardly touching his dinner—linguini pasta in a marinara sauce. His waistline was shrinking, and Barbara had no idea why. When she asked him about it, he sloughed her off.

She turned her attention back to the others, heard Larry ask Tom if Arrow had truly closed up in Canada.

"Yes … for good," Tom said bitterly.

"So how will this affect you?" Larry asked. He had friends in the distribution field and knew how the least shift at retail impacted their businesses.

"*Merde!* In a big way," Denise broke in, not hiding her distress.

"We don't know for sure," Tom said, trying to soften the news. "I went to see our lawyer back in Toronto. There's hope our debt will be recovered."

"All of it?" Larry asked optimistically.

"Not very likely," Denise again interrupted. "If we get a quarter of it back, I'll be delighted. Half and I'll be ecstatic."

Barbara found Denise's fiery temper enticing. Not for the first time, she wondered what it would be like to embrace her

French-Canadian passion; to make love to the woman without any inhibitions whatsoever.

* * *

Debbie Stafford made her way back to the table, hoping upon hope that the watch would miraculously be there, next to her dinner plate.

It was nowhere in sight.

"Are you okay?" she heard her husband ask.

"I'm fine," she lied, sat down, and began to dig into the pasta she'd ordered, fettuccine in an aioli sauce.

"It must be cold by now," Larry pointed out.

Debbie flinched, finding his comment embarrassing, especially in front of their friends.

"Should we get them to heat it up?"

Shut up! Shut up! Shut up! she almost said out loud.

"Dear..."

She was about to acknowledge him, when a muted gasp from across the table drew her attention.

Denise Gerigk was glaring at her iPhone, a shocked look on her face.

"What is it?" Debbie asked.

Denise finally made the announcement, her voice somewhat shaken: "A news bulletin from the local CBS affiliate: Jill Derbyshire was found ... bludgeoned to death with a golf club."

16

Earlier the same day

It was mid-afternoon when I approached the Derbyshire house and parked. The sighting of a suspicious vehicle had been called in by a neighbor. I was tied up at an AA meeting, so I'd asked Brad Pedersen to investigate. The minute he uncovered the murder he'd phoned me, and I was on my way.

I stepped up to the door only to find that Sara Churchill had beaten me to the crime scene. She greeted me without much enthusiasm, still displaying anger over my behavior last night.

"Been here long?" I asked.

"Not really."

I indicated the orange crime scene tape, cordoning off the great room. "Nothing's been touched, I take it?"

"Only the bare essentials—things my staff and your staff had to get to."

I bent beneath the tape and approached the body. There were three wounds to the back of Jill Derbyshire's head, each deep and severe. Massive blood spatter stained the wall beyond. The woman never stood a chance. She'd most likely turned away from her assailant when the first blow with the golf club had been struck. It would have killed her or at least knocked her unconscious. The second finished the job if she wasn't already dead. The third, I figured, was insurance. The blood-stained golf club was lying by Mrs. Derbyshire's feet. A partially obscured nametag high on the shaft indicated it belonged to her.

"I think this was less personal than the others," I speculated. "Sinclair and Gladstone faced their killer and for an instant saw what was coming. But Derbyshire had no idea. If it's the same guy, he might be feeling less sure of himself, might even be troubled by guilt."

"Not guilt." Sara became animated. "More a disassociation. Our killer might be losing control. Too anxious to kill to wait for his victim to turn and look at him."

"What about the victims themselves? The fact that all lived in this one neighborhood of Augusta? We've spoken to neighbors, friends and relatives. Then I personally traced former residents going back five years. Nothing there. I expanded my search to the service men and women. I followed the theory that all three victims hurt someone in some way, perhaps complained to someone's boss and had them fired."

"And?"

"Not one suspect. At least not yet. There are a few hundred interviews yet to be done. Meanwhile, the murders are piling up … and I can't seem to stop them."

Sara turned toward me. "You sound defeated."

"Wouldn't you be?"

"Don't give up, Miles. You'll catch whoever's doing this." She glanced at her watch. "Oh-oh. Sorry, I've got to go."

As I watched her leave, I again wondered what had come between us.

* * *

Once Sara's SUV was out of sight, I locked up the house with the spare key I had in my possession and headed next door.

Mrs. Harding was the one who'd called in the report about a suspicious car in the Derbyshire driveway. Close to ninety years old, she'd come to Florida to retire in anticipated safety. Instead, the spate of homicides had her living in abject fear for her life.

I knocked on the door. I could tell she was scrutinizing me through the peep hole. I held up my badge. She recognized me finally, opened the door and put the baseball bat she was holding back into the nearby umbrella canister.

Despite the warm temperature, she was wearing a wool dress that fell to her ankles. Her house had a closed-in feel to it, the air stale as if the windows and doors had not been opened for months. I followed her to the great room where we both took a seat across from each other on individual upholstered chairs. The furniture could have been as old as she was, mostly with faux-wood trim in dark shades of brown.

"Your fellow deputy told me what happened," she said before I could ask anything. "I knew something was wrong. I should have called it in sooner. But I was worried about making a fool of myself. Mrs. Derbyshire was a wonderful neighbor. She was always doing nice things for me. Carrying in my groceries, helping me take out the garbage. I can't imagine…" Tears flowed. She pulled out a tissue from her housedress pocket and blew her nose. "…what I'll do without her."

I gave her time to compose herself, then asked if she remembered anything else about the car.

"No. I don't."

"What kind was it?"

"A white one," Mrs. Harding replied, proud of herself.

"Make? Model?" I prompted.

"I have no idea," she said, momentarily stumped; then, "but it was one of those modern things you see these days, with fancy curves in the body."

My hope deflated. White cars in Florida with fancy curves would number in the hundreds of thousands. "Is there anything else you can remember? The license plate, perhaps?"

"The license plate?"

"Yes. Please think, Mrs. Harding."

"N…No." She shook her head solemnly, then brightened. "One. It had the number one in the middle of the plate. Or … was it a seven? My eyesight isn't too good, you know."

"Can you be more specific, ma'am?"

The look she gave me was so regretful I felt sorry for her. "I don't know if I can. I wish I could do more. I really do…"

"That's okay," I said, afraid she might start crying again. "You've been very helpful. Honestly." I took out one of my cards, stood, and handed it to her. "I have to go now, Mrs. Harding. But if you remember anything else, especially a few of the other numbers in the license plate, please call me. "

* * *

I went home but couldn't sleep, not after answering phone calls from Sheriff Norman as well as Mayors Hillier and Torbram.

This most recent murder was sending everyone into a panic. Until now, the sheriff had given me as much leeway as he could afford, but there were zero results. Even after hundreds of interviews, no one knew anything. No one could provide a lead. Frustration lingered like a meal gone bad, constantly tracing a rancid path through my stomach.

A meeting had been called for first thing in the morning. Sheriff Norman had given me a heads-up, but I still hadn't figured out the best way to handle the situation. *Should I show my irritation or not? Be diplomatic or go on the offensive?*

They marched into my office; first the sheriff, tall and broad-shouldered, his stature seldom wavering, followed by my two least favorite mayors. Then last, a man I'd never met but who needed no introduction: Hank Broderick, my predecessor. Early-fifties, hazel eyes, average height and weight, brown hair turning to gray.

Once they were seated the sheriff cut to the chase: "Miles, lucky for us the Tampa Sheriff's Department has a light caseload at the moment. Until our murders have been solved, I've brought in Hank Broderick, on loan, to help out. He has extensive knowledge of Bonita Springs and the wherewithal to probe into places you may not be familiar with."

The man reached out to shake my hand. I immediately disliked him. The look on his face was smug, and he held my gaze longer than normal, as if waiting for me to blink first. It was childish, but I refused to give him the satisfaction, even after he leaned back in his seat.

I'd suspected this was coming. Mayor Hillier wanted his friend back onboard and had gotten his way. *Chalk up one for the asshole.* The last thing I needed was a gunslinger interfering with my investigation.

"Gentlemen," I said, "no offense, but my men have this. They've been working around the clock and are getting close to an arrest. It will take too long to bring an outsider up to speed. *Particularly a phony like this guy,* I held back adding.

It was my pride talking, of course. We weren't getting closer. While it was true that my team had been working around the clock, we'd come up empty. More importantly, we still couldn't establish a clear motive for the murders.

"Hold on here!" Mayor Hillier flew into a rage. "Are you that egotistical you'd deny professional help when it's offered to you?"

I ignored the man's comments and turned to Broderick. "Hank—you've been away from this office for what? Eight years? Surely you don't expect to step back in and carry on where you left off, do you?"

"Of course, he does," Mayor Torbram butted in. "You're not the only one with expertise around here. Hank's *earned* his reputation."

"What reputa—" I started to say when Broderick stood and glared at me.

"Don't know what you've heard, but I'm no rookie around these parts. Seems to me you've had enough time to solve these murders, yet you've got nothing to show for it. Nada. While all it should take is good police work. Something you may not be familiar with." Instead of taking his seat again, he remained standing, letting the challenge hang in the air.

This a-hole wants a dual? I scoffed inwardly. That's his game?

I was a nanosecond away from calling Hank's bluff when Sheriff Norman spoke up. "Miles—Broderick's been brought in to be of assistance to you. I need you to give him a chance. He knows the ropes. It's not like he might corrupt the evidence."

I opened my mouth to speak, then decided against it. The sheriff had his own agenda, and I realized that Broderick—for whatever reason— had Mayor Hillier as well as the sheriff in his corner as an ally. *Okay. Let's just see how this interesting drama plays out.*

17

February 5

At 8:00 p.m. Frank Sinclair, dressed in a dark green shirt and navy shorts, bellied up to the bar and ordered a Manhattan. The sound system played unobtrusive jazz in the background; something by Winston Marsalis. The lighting was exceptionally dim. Frank could barely see who was seated on either side of him.

 The Zanzibar was a private club located on the outskirts of Naples and fronted a manmade lake. The exterior of the one-story building was purposely nondescript: dark red-bricked with a slate-shingle roof and windows that remained shuttered at all times. Few neighbors were aware of what went on inside. The parking lot was fenced-in and required a keycard to gain access. Dense foliage camouflaged the entranceway.

 Frank counted only two other gentleman and three women. But it was still early. All were middle-aged or older. Private, leather-furnished booths lining the walls were currently empty. Frank knew that most of the club's members were married or recently widowed or divorced. Their motivation for joining was more the need for sex than companionship.

He smiled to himself. Years ago, this place would have been known as a "swingers club" or "key club." Today, there was little point in stereotyping. It was what it was. The fact that many spouses of the members were left in the dark was beside the point. The thought of their mental anguish—should they discover the club's existence—didn't enter the picture. Like an itch that had to be scratched, some urges had to be fulfilled.

Frank flashed a look at the woman on his right, two stools over. *Barbara?* he almost said aloud. He took a closer look. The resemblance to Barbara Miller was remarkable. He was reminded of the last time he'd been with Barbara, and the reason for not wanting to see her again.

They'd just made love, of a sort, and Frank couldn't quite figure out what had happened. There was no denying he'd been turned on by her. But he'd also felt left out, as if this had been Barbara's erotic experience solely for herself. She'd marginalized him, turned him into a bit player, employed to perform a service and nothing more.

Frank lost interest after that, stopped taking her calls, simply froze her out. *Next?*

* * *

"I haven't seen you here before." The woman's smile was flirtatious.

"I don't come here often." *Primarily when I'm horny and desperate.*

She extended her hand. "Melanie."

"George," Frank lied, figuring she'd done the same. He briefly shook her hand and let go.

She slid over to the adjacent stool and leaned toward him.

Frank observed that she not only had Barbara Miller's looks, she was approximately the same age—late forties, early fifties. Too good-looking and young to be hanging around a place like this. *Most likely's a story here*, Frank figured.

"You live close by?" she asked.

"Close enough. Yourself?"

"Near Pelican Bay."

"I'm somewhat north of you," he lied again. "In West Bay Club."

"Ah. Too far to go."

"Is it?"

"I think so. Why drive all that distance when there are alternatives?"

"You're almost empty," he said, indicating her glass. "Can I get you another?"

She nodded. "Sure."

"What's your pleasure?"

"Gin rocks. With a twist."

Frank placed the order with the female bartender, plus another Manhattan for himself.

Melanie was wearing a low-cut burgundy blouse and black pants that were so tight they appeared to pinch her skin. Her dark hair was done up in a double-tiered bun. Frank was already imagining undoing it, watching the hair cascade down her neck and onto her ample breasts.

"What do you do?" he asked to keep the conversation moving. "Or what did you do—in your previous life?"

"How do you know I've had one?"

Frank smiled. "Everyone's had one."

"What do you do?"

"Absolutely nothing."

"Previously?"

"Nothing at all."

She playfully slapped his arm.

"What?" Frank said, feigning surprise. "Isn't everyone in Florida living a life of fantasy?"

Melanie shrugged. "Not everyone, I'm sure."

"Husband?" Frank tossed out casually.

"Wife?" Melanie countered.

Both smiled demurely and the stage was set. Neither was going to tell the truth about anything.

* * *

Frank followed Melanie to her house in his car.

There was a circular driveway. And a FOR SALE sign on the front lawn. Melanie led the way, opening an oversized wood door with stained-glass panels and ushering him inside.

Frank found the foyer magnificent. Cathedral ceiling, brass chandelier, with statues and pop art paintings lining both walls, and a view that led to a lanai with a multi-colored spotlight that illuminated a waterfall splashing into a pool.

"One Manhattan, coming up," Melanie said, pointing toward the corridor on his right. "Go into the den and make yourself comfortable. I'll only be a minute."

Frank followed her directions, ending up in a mahogany-paneled room with a bookcase, television set, and leather couch. He kicked off his sandals before walking on the carpeted floor and took a seat.

In no time at all she was standing in front of him, proffering his drink while holding her own in her other hand. She'd changed into a frilly nightgown; so transparent she might as well have been naked.

Frank tapped the couch and she sat down next to him. In between sips of their drinks they necked like teenagers on a first date. Words seemed superfluous. Melanie was in no hurry and Frank didn't mind. Soon after he'd drained his glass, Frank felt the call of nature, and he asked to use the bathroom.

She pointed it out to him.

Inside, he observed the gold-plate, almost used to excess, on the frame of the mirrored vanity, the taps in the sink, the trim on the towel rack.

Frank relieved himself, then washed down his precautionary Viagra with a gulp of tap water.

The lights had been dimmed in the den when he returned, but Frank could see that the couch had been pulled into a bed. Melanie was leaning against one of the pillows, nightgown partially open, exposing more than her thighs.

Frank stripped and slipped in beside her, his cock now at full mast. But something odd was happening in his head; thoughts became scrambled. It wasn't the booze itself. Frank could hold his liquor; always had. A dizziness gave way to the sense of falling. He was losing his balance even though he was lying in bed.

"My ... drink," he managed to say, realizing too late that he'd been roofied. "What did you..."

* * *

A flash of Melanie's breasts. A tangle of arms and legs. Frank was positioned inside her, that much he knew, when a man's voice came to him, catching him off guard. He wanted to comment; his tongue felt glued to the roof of his mouth.

"You are with friends," Melanie was saying just as an engorged penis entered him from behind.

Shock gave way to dismay. Frank didn't want this. But he'd been drugged, and it was working. Leaving him defenseless and unable to resist, his body accepting the unimaginable.

Through it all, he heard the sound of a camera clicking away.

18

February 7

Late afternoon, a corkboard sat on an easel against the near wall of my office. Present were the only men I trusted, Brad Pedersen and Scott Wellington; both in uniform but with their hats removed. Hank Broderick hadn't been invited. The clock was ticking. If something didn't break soon, I'd be out of a job.

"Let's review the facts." I pointed toward the upper left-hand corner of the board, then paused. The eight-by-ten color crime scene photograph of Cathy Sinclair emphasized the brutal nature of her murder.

"DOD—January 4th," Brad Pedersen said, reading the date of death stamped beneath the woman's picture. "Blunt-force trau-ma to the head. Before nightfall. No forced entry. She was alone at the time."

"And?" I pushed.

"Her husband was out of town."

"That's right," I confirmed. "Or so he said. Our investigation couldn't prove otherwise. But he isn't off the hook. At least, not yet. The suspicion of adultery still hangs over his head. What better reason to get rid of a wife than that?"

I turned once more to the board. "Victim number two, Cynthia Gladstone, sixty-three years old."

"DOD—January 17th," Scott Wellington said. "Same cause—blunt force trauma. Same time of day as the first homicide. Alone in the house. Husband out on an errand. But he's proving to be beyond reproach. I've looked into every facet of his life. Couldn't find a dent. Not a tax bill unpaid. No hint whatsoever of suspicious activity in his past."

"Okay, that leaves us with the third and latest victim—Jill Derbyshire." I stepped closer to the corkboard and tapped her photograph. The woman seldom looked her age until now.

"Bludgeoned to death with her own golf club," Pedersen stated ruefully. "January 25. Just before nightfall. Husband, Jack, alibied up at an AT&T reunion. He flew back to town the minute his wife's murder was discovered. And he's still in pretty bad shape. However, our investigation turned up a financial problem the Derbyshire's were facing, something that could have ruined them. Jack is the beneficiary of his wife's million-dollar insurance policy, which I find a little too convenient."

"You're right," I agreed. "These little peccadilloes, so to speak, with at least two of the husbands, give us something to consider. Substantiated alibis notwithstanding, nothing should be overlooked." I took a few steps back. "Let's move on," I said, directing their attention to an entirely different set of photographs.

"Harold Brown, electrician with Florida Power and Light, is one suspect." I paused and pointed to his picture on the board, that of a handsome man in his late-forties. "We know he doesn't have a credible alibi so he's worth a further look. And then there's Turk Lagerfeld, technician with Comcast. Brad—you said something was off when you re-interviewed him?"

"Yes, and he had a vibe coming off him. Deep rooted anger or bitterness. Physically, he's an imposing guy. Not someone you'd want to meet alone in a dark alley. A definite hatred of the opposite sex. I'm investigating his background."

"Good." I looked at my watch. "That's enough for today. But there's one other thing I need to mention." *Be careful*, a voice in my head warned, *you're on shaky ground*. "Should Hank Broderick ask questions about our investigation, you refer him to me posthaste. Don't divulge any information to him whatsoever."

* * *

I waited for both men to leave, then leaned back in my chair and cupped my hands behind my head. My gut was telling me that the only true suspect we had was Cathy's husband—Frank Sinclair. I theorized that his plan all along was to murder his wife. Or, more likely, he'd paid an accomplice to kill her—a hit-man-for-hire. A professional clever enough to leave no evidence behind.

I'd solved some major crimes in my day, especially in Chicago. Murder for personal gain, for revenge, or simply for the thrill of it all. Perps who were more intelligent than most, or plainly psychotic. I'd seen every type. And I wasn't going to let this bastard—be it Frank Sinclair or someone else—get away with it.

19

February 13

Her car was a blue C-class Mercedes. Not a popular color in Southwest Florida, where white dominated. But Bill Miller wouldn't have had a problem following his wife no matter what color of car she was driving. Barbara tended to go slow. Turtle slow. Bill figured he could pull over and nap for five minutes and still be able to keep up with her.

In and out of traffic. From 41, to Bonita Beach Boulevard, to 75. Then south for a few miles until she reached the Immokalee exit. West from there for ten minutes until Barbara pulled into a non-gated community.

Bill hung back. His wife knew his car, of course, even if there were a disproportionate number of Bentleys in this part of Florida compared to the rest of the country.

He pulled in behind a delivery truck and parked. He was half a block down from the house Barbara was visiting. From where he sat, he had a clear line of sight. He observed his wife in the driveway fishing for something in her car, most likely her purse.

She finally stepped out. Bill couldn't positively tell from the distance he was at, but he was fairly sure she was wearing a smile of anticipation. There was even a sprightliness in her step as she approached the front door.

The minute she entered the house, Bill put his car in gear and moved closer, until he was near enough to identify whoever might show up next.

He turned off the motor and went to lean back, when he doubled over in pain. He punched the dash as hard as he could. Then again and again, until shockwaves ran up and down his arm.

He'd been holding off making the appointment with his doctor. Bill suspected his cancer had metastasized, but he didn't want to know, even though the pain was getting worse. This wasn't what he'd envisioned for his retirement. Back in his twenties his moniker had been "Ironman Bill." He'd had the world by the balls and thought he'd live forever. Now he was in ill health and his financial world was crumbling, with too many losses and not enough new suckers to keep the money rolling in.

"Fuck!" he swore aloud. The hurt wouldn't subside. He held on to the steering wheel with all his might. *Breathe in through your nose, out through your mouth*, a doctor had counseled. And he tried it … didn't do a bit of good.

He electronically adjusted his seat, leaned back, and brought his legs up. He was contemplating returning home when a red Ford Focus pulled into the driveway.

That's not Frank Sinclair's car. Bill recognized June Adams immediately, the assistant pro at Bonita Palms, as she got out of the vehicle. *Why is SHE meeting with my wife?*

His cheeks flushed. *To buy a house, you idiot!* Here he was, thinking the worst of Barbara, when she was actually working.

He started the car, then hesitated. What if this was only the first of two meetings his wife had arranged? Number one being business, number two pleasure?

He shut off the motor and turned the radio on to 101.9. A song by a new artist he didn't know was playing and he liked it. His favorite country station seldom disappointed.

* * *

Bill nodded off. Half in, half out of dozing, he heard women's laughter. He opened his eyes, checked his watch, and was surprised to see that two hours had gone by. The women were just exiting the home, giggling like schoolgirls. *An awfully long time spent on looking at a house,* Bill figured.

Both women hesitated, embraced, looked lovingly into each other's eyes, then passionately kissed in the open doorway.

Bill recoiled in shock.

The kiss lingered, with tongues teasing.

He wanted to vomit. He wanted to laugh. Or cry. He wanted to take his wife's neck in his hands and wrench her head off her body. It was one thing to discover her affair with Frank Sinclair. But this? Cheating with a woman? Not simply a cuckold. *Good God in Heaven!* This made him … he couldn't even think of a word for it.

After June Adams got into her car and drove off, Bill fired up the Bentley and floored it, tires squealing. He didn't slow for yellow lights turning to red, barely able to focus.

As if on automatic pilot, the car brought him home to Augusta. Bill left the vehicle in the driveway, hopped out and slammed the door. Once inside the house he made a beeline for the master bedroom.

A few of Barbara's favorite things rested on the bureau next to her side of the bed. A musical jewelry box with a windup ballerina, an acrylic flower grouping, and a delicate Venus de Milo glass statue.

Bill grabbed the statue and his rage propelled him into Barbara's bathroom. He heaved the statue—an antique his wife had found in Istanbul—at the mirror. There was a tremendous popping sound as the glass shattered, shards of statue and mirror flying in all directions, almost catching Bill in the face as he ducked.

Out of the house and back into his Bentley, Bill felt no satisfaction from what he'd done; none whatsoever. Frustration and anger were so deeply rooted, he realized it wasn't likely to go away anytime soon, not unless he achieved the revenge he so desperately craved; payback that was long overdue.

20

February 16

Mayor Hillier confronted me in my office at 9:00 a.m. Without saying a word he waved both local newspapers—one from Fort Myers, the other from Bonita Springs—each called the *News Press*. I was seated at my desk, but even from an odd angle I could make out the headlines.

SHERIFF'S DEPARTMENT AT A LOSS!
SERIAL KILLER STILL ON THE LOOSE!

I held back my anger. The intention of the press was to sell newspapers. I couldn't fault them for doing their job. But it was the mayor who got to me; his desire to assign blame.

Sweat was already dripping off the man's pudgy cheeks, his hands in constant motion. Like a litany, he listed the lack of results, harping back to Cathy Sinclair's murder and describing it in minute detail. "My constituents are fed up," he continued. "I hear by the grapevine that a petition's been started, calling for my removal from office. Me! When you're the deputy sheriff! When it's *you* who should've had this investigation wrapped up long before now!"

I was about to suggest that the man take a seat before having a coronary when he did exactly that, then removed a handkerchief from his jacket pocket and wiped his brow.

"You leave me no choice," he said as if this was actually difficult for him. "Change was inevitable. As of this moment, you'll no longer fill the role of lead investigator. That position has been transferred to Hank Broderick. It'll be up to him to utilize your services as he sees fit."

Sonofabitch! I suspected this was coming but was still blown away by his audacity. "No," I said calmly.

"What's that?"

"This isn't a decision *you* can make."

"Oh? Wanna bet? It's already been made."

* * *

I picked up the phone and called Sara Churchill. She'd been less cool to me lately. I'd racked my brain trying to recall what had happened that night at her house, even went so far as to ask her about it. All she'd say was that I shouldn't pretend I didn't know.

She answered on the third ring. "Hello?"

"How about lunch?"

"Sorry, I'm tied up."

"I need to ask you something."

"Can't you ask it over the phone?"

There was nothing to ask; I just wanted her company. "Not really."

"Then let's make it another time."

"Sure."

I came to my feet and took the stairs, hurtling downwards

like a man on a mission. I had to get out of there. Out of my office, out of the building; away from everyone.

I walked briskly with no destination in mind. The first restaurant I passed had a large Heineken sign in the window.

One beer might do the trick, I figured. The next showcased Bud Lite.

The longer I walked, the worse it got. From beer to bourbon to vodka: advertisements everywhere, teasing. I turned and retraced my steps.

* * *

Late afternoon I drove out to a small church off Daniel's Parkway to an AA meeting with an open invitation sponsored by the Salvation Army of Fort Myers.

We were a baker's dozen including myself, gathered in the recreation room. A fifty-something-year-old woman was the first to speak. Thin, brown unruly hair, turtle-shelled glasses, she sounded miserable, talking about her kids being taken away from her.

After fifteen minutes, an African American gentleman in his late sixties or early seventies spoke of the demon rum. "I had the bottle to my lips," he said. "I knew better than to drink, but the devil had his way with me…" and he droned on in misery.

The next person to speak was a man around forty, with full head of dirty brown, uncombed hair and a deep, baritone voice. "I fell off the wagon and went on a bender that lasted over a month, maybe longer. Finally, I pulled myself together and sobered up … completely. But my wife left me anyway. Took the only people that matter to me—my son and daughter. So why even try to stay sober? There's no justice in this world. Might as well drink as not."

A few people in the room started talking at once, offering suggestions and words of encouragement. The moderator had to remind them they were not supposed to try and give advice. By now, I'd stopped listening. It wasn't only the stories that were getting me down. My mind was in a fragile state and I had no idea how to fix it.

* * *

Night had fallen by the time I left the church. There was a haze in the sky foreboding bad weather for tomorrow. I didn't once pause to consider where I was going.

Inside Costco, I drifted over to the one area of the warehouse I had no business being. Rum and scotch. Vodka, gin, Canadian whisky. Bottles positioned like impeccable centurions, row upon row, for the most or least discriminating taste.

The forty-ouncer of Jack Daniels was in my hands; it took willpower not to open it on the spot, take a long pull, and once more feel the glorious sensation in my throat.

I headed toward the checkout, my head buzzing. I paid, then started for the exit. There were half a dozen people waiting in line in front of me. My conscience tweaked; I ignored it. My receipt was verified and I was waved through.

At home, I changed into a tee and jeans and strolled into the bathroom. The plastic container of Narvia was in the top drawer. I carried it and the bottle of Jack into the great room, where I lowered myself onto the sofa, placed both items down on the shag rug by my feet.

I hadn't touched a pill in three days. This was the second time recently that I'd tried going without. It was more than what it did to my stomach. I'd been experiencing blackouts lately, periods of time where I couldn't remember where I was or what I'd done.

Which poison is better? I questioned.

I grew up in an Irish/American family. Unlike others of our heritage, my father seldom drank. The truth was, I had no one to blame but myself.

My eyes drifted back and forth from the pill container to the bottle of Jack. And I knew—deep inside—what the correct choice should be. But something tugged, pulling me in a direction I didn't want to go.

I took hold of the bottle. Before I could change my mind, I had it open.

21

February 18

Debbie Stafford locked herself in her bedroom and glanced at her watch. The same Cartier she thought she had lost when she'd arrived for dinner at Cirella's almost three weeks ago, only to discover it lying on the counter by the bathroom sink after she'd gotten home later the same night. She counted ten more minutes just to be sure. Her husband might have forgotten something, or he might be planning to surprise her. She didn't want to take that chance. A little while longer wouldn't matter.

She was out of sorts today, more than usual. Her morning had begun with a sharp pain in her right leg. Why it always had to be the one on the right was a puzzle to her; more like a burn, it was distracting. Pennsaid, her anti-inflammatory medication, usually did the trick. She squeezed out twenty drops and massaged the clear liquid into her aching limb.

Then she caught her image in the mirror and reeled back. *Hag*, she thought. Black hair hanging in clotted strings. Cheeks wrinkled and bloated. Cracked lips begging for a coat of Chapstick. Tired eyes with no hint of warmth let alone life.

Debbie stood stock-still, staring at herself. She filled a glass with water, placed two of her Narvia pills in her mouth, and washed them down with her obligatory six sips.

* * *

Larry was waiting in the reception area of Dr. Susan Kline, an Alzheimer's specialist. The doctor had come recommended. Larry felt guilty about going behind his wife's back, but felt he had no choice. For weeks, he'd been trying to come up with a reason for Debbie's behavior; for her mood swings, for the way she was letting herself go to seed.

"Mr. Stafford?"

He looked up.

The receptionist beckoned him to follow her.

The office was spacious. Picture windows allowed the sun to stream in and fill the room with light. Diplomas hung in glass frames behind the desk.

The doctor—barely five feet, if he had to guess; middle-aged and blonde— introduced herself and shook his hand. "I understand you're here about your wife?" she said once they'd taken their seats.

"Yes, I—" He was stuck for words.

"Does she know about your visit?"

"Huh?"

"Is she aware that you are here today?"

Larry felt his cheeks burning. "No, I—"

"No need to explain," the doctor assured him. "What's your wife's name, Mr. Stafford?"

"Debra. Or Debbie."

"And what makes you think Debbie has Alzheimer's disease?"

"I don't know that she does—" he began, then froze.

"Go on."

"Well—"

"Look, perhaps it would help if I asked you a few simple questions. Would that be alright with you?"

"Yes, of course." His discomfort eased.

"Does your wife respond to her own name?"

"Yes, she does."

"Does she know what day of the week it is?"

"Yes."

"The time of day?"

"Yes."

"The month we are in?"

"Yes."

"Her address?"

"Uh-huh."

"Her phone number?"

He nodded.

"How about her date of birth?"

"Yes," he said, "as far as I know."

"Is she forgetful?"

"Sometimes … not often," he corrected himself for accuracy.

"Does she seem mentally unavailable to you?"

"In what way?"

"Does she spend many hours brooding? In a fugue state? Unaware of her surroundings?"

"Yes!" *Now we're getting somewhere.* "And lately she seems possessed by God. Hears Him talking to her sometimes."

Dr. Kline scribbled in her notepad. "How about her maiden name?"

"She knows it."

"Does she ever forget your name?"

"No."

"Your date of birth?"

"Uh-uh."

"The name of our president?"

"She knows who he is," Larry said. And he was convinced: Debbie no more had Alzheimer's disease than he did.

Dr. Kline put down her pen. "Mr. Stafford, oftentimes we notice a change in the ones we're closest to and it worries us. In your wife's case, it's appears to be her religion. According to you, she's far more fervent about it now than she was before. But I don't believe it's harming anyone. Is it?"

Larry shrugged. "No, I guess not."

"Well, perhaps there are other factors motivating this kind of behavior."

"Like what?"

"A change in your relationship? The way you communicate with one another?"

He became embarrassed. "I … don't think so."

The doctor pounced on the vagueness of his answer. "May I suggest you give it more thought? In the meantime, I will gladly meet with your wife. But from the answers you've given me, I don't believe there's an indicator for Alzheimer's disease. Bringing her here might be a waste of time and money. I'll leave it up to you to decide."

* * *

On the drive home Larry reviewed the questions he'd been asked along with his answers. *If Debbie doesn't have Alzheimer's disease, what does she have?* Doctor Kline insinuated he could be partly to blame; something to do with their relationship, or the way he was communicating with her.

Perhaps he hadn't expressed himself properly? Debbie's recent behavior had nothing to do with him. She'd gone over the top; listening to voices, speaking to a God only she could hear.

He reached their house and parked in the driveway next to his wife's car. He walked in and called out his hello.

No answer.

"Deb?"

Nothing.

He called her name again. Still no reply, he moved toward the master bedroom, thinking his wife might be taking a nap.

The empty room ratcheted up his concern. He searched the other rooms, finally knocking on the door to Debbie's office.

No response.

He turned the handle and poked his head in. She wasn't there. He was about to leave when he heard a muffled groan coming from behind the bookcase at the back. Larry was aware of his wife's hidden alcove. He rushed forward, removed the Bible on the center shelf of the bookcase and hit the switch. The bookcase popped apart. The lights in the alcove were ablaze. Debbie's body was lying prone at the base of Christ's statue. He rushed to her side and searched for a pulse; found it, but it was weak. He whipped out his cell, dialed 911, then turned back to his wife and began to apply CPR.

22

February 21

"You've already had your damn vacation!" Hank Broderick said from the doorway to my office. He entered and took a seat.

"So?" I said.

"You won't be paid."

"I know that." Getting paid was the furthest thing from my mind.

"And this will go against your record."

That surprised me. "For taking a leave of absence?"

"Now—in the middle of a murder investigation? Yes, of course."

I leaned back in my chair.

"Well?"

"I still need the time off."

"And I need you here, on the case."

"But I've been demoted. Remember? You're the one now in charge."

"You weren't demoted. Just asked to step aside."

"That's the same thing."

"No, it isn't."

I sat there and stared at Hank, giving him a little of his own medicine, refusing to blink first. Three weeks of working with the man only drove us further apart. It wasn't that I didn't try. Broderick was every bit as self-centered as I believed he would be when we first met. Not purely egotistical but a phony, someone who thought too highly of himself, someone who talked down to everyone, especially the men under my command.

However, with Broderick now being my superior, I'd had no choice but to send my request for time off through to him via email less than an hour ago. And here he was.

"I need every able-bodied person available for duty," he said, breaking the silence.

I let him stew for an extra minute, then said with finality, "I'll only be gone five days."

Broderick stood. "You want your time off, take it! But you better hope that another murder doesn't occur in your absence!" He turned and stomped out of my office.

* * *

The drive was long and tedious. I had lots of time to mull over my relationship with Hank Broderick. As far as I was concerned, I saw no evidence of a brilliant analytical mind. If anything, I was yet to see why Sheriff Norman and Mayor Hillier held him in such high esteem.

I was using my personal car—a year-old Chevy; I'd been loyal to the one brand all my life. I'd started off on I-75 heading north, keeping more or less to the speed limit.

I made frequent stops, for the restroom as well as coffee. The first motel I chose cost eighty dollars. It'd been a while since I'd stayed in one and it felt strange. The room was of average size with a musty smell to it. Sleep was slow in coming.

The following morning, I had breakfast and was back on the road by 9:00 a.m. I turned on the radio and searched the dial. All I could get was static; it was too isolated an area for anything coherent.

A horn honked. I'd lost focus and had drifted into the passing lane. I quickly corrected, then slowed down.

The second motel I picked had a television that didn't work and a phone that was out of order.

* * *

It took three days to get to my destination. Upon arrival, I made a detour and purchased flowers. Then I left my car with the doorman at my hotel—a Hilton downtown.

In the morning I was on my way before nine. The wind was one thing about Chicago I'd never gotten used to; and the cold. After living in Florida, they both felt much worse and I was glad I'd brought a coat.

Traffic stalled. I arrived at the cemetery after a drive forty minutes too long. The plot I'd purchased for my wife and son was in a newer section. I parked as near as I could.

The temperature was in the mid-thirties. There was no snow on the ground, yet the air felt damp. There were no other visitors close by.

I approached the gravesite and placed the flowers I'd picked up the day before at the double tombstone. I said a prayer, then lowered myself to a sitting position and crossed my legs.

The reason why I came here, why I *had* to be here today, was to honor the anniversary of my wife's passing. That, as well as the fact that I was teetering on a precipice; still unnerved from my demotion and its aftereffects, still upset that something I couldn't remember—and she wouldn't say—had come between Sara and me. Most of all, I was very much bothered that my willpower could've become so diminished I'd actually purchase a bottle of Jack Daniels and seriously think about drinking it.

I'd held that open bottle in my hand for too many minutes, then started to put it to my lips; a nanosecond away from a relapse; a nanosecond away from destroying my life for good.

I had no idea what stopped me, but I thanked my lucky stars that something did. Some last vestige of conscience caused me to march into the kitchen, tilt the damn bottle, and pour its entire contents down the drain.

I didn't feel relief afterwards; only shame.

* * *

"I'm sorry," I said, my eyes fixed on the tombstone, apologizing simultaneously to my son and Alice. The words sounded trite and I grew embarrassed. An involuntary sound escaped my lips, part sigh, part groan. I closed my eyes and envisioned my wife as she lay dying; how emaciated she'd looked, the sickly smell of her shallow breath. All because of me.

A lifetime of penitence wouldn't be enough. And sitting there in my personal funk, I was hit by a stark premonition. My demotion at work was only the beginning; I was soon going to have to face a lot worse.

23

February 22

"*Tabernac!*" Denise Gerigk swore.

Her neck again, on the right side. She tried to keep as still as possible. But the dish of hors d'oeuvres she held was getting heavy. She slowly moved toward the great room and set the plate down on the coffee table; waited for the pain to ease up.

Denise looked at her watch: almost 1:30 p.m. Their mid-week bridge game had been switched to Saturday and it was her turn to host. She had only a few minutes before the others would arrive.

At the best of times she was restrained from moving her neck without also moving her shoulders. They either worked in unison, as a single unit, or she suffered the worst spasms imaginable. Whenever she forgot—like a minute ago—her neck seized up and sent her a vicious reminder.

Mind over matter, she told herself, and purposely put a bounce in her step, returning to the kitchen to round up the balance of appetizers.

***

They all showed up at once. Barbara Miller, her usual showy self, in a tight lavender blouse, mauve short-shorts, and high heels. And two women recently conscripted into the bridge group as replacements for Denise's murdered friends: Carol Monaghan, brown hair done up in a bun, wearing a navy pants suit. And Joan Ward, a sixty-six-year-old petite blonde dressed in a black and white golf outfit. Joan was a well-liked neighbor who'd just returned from Madison, Wisconsin where she'd spent three months looking after, then burying her mother, who suffered from heart disease. Denise led the way into the great room where the bridge table and chairs were set up. Two decks of cards—one red-backed, the other blue—in opposite corners.

The women took their seats and Denise pointed out the abundance of snacks she'd laid out on the adjacent coffee table: two kinds of potato chips, smoked salmon, devilled eggs, guacamole, a variety of imported cheeses, pita bread and a humus dip. "Help yourself," she said. "The hot stuff will be served later."

"God, I hope not," Barbara Miller objected. "You're going overboard again, always trying to fatten us up."

It was true, Denise reflected. Not the fattening up part, but she *was* trying to go that one step beyond. Not to show off, more to prove she was an equal. In truth, she'd always felt inferior to these women. Their showy homes, their wealth, were far and beyond anything she and Tom had accomplished. Somehow, she couldn't live down the feeling of inferiority, and this was her way of making up for it.

The bridge game commenced; Barbara was her first partner. By the third round Denise was ready to call it quits. She'd had bad luck before, but this was ridiculous. *"Colin,"* she swore under her breath.

"What's that?" Carol Monaghan asked. "Babbling in French once more? You do realize the rest of us can't understand a word you're saying, don't you?"

Denise smiled. "Better that you don't," and went back to studying her hopeless hand.

By the time they changed partners Denise had opened the second bottle of wine. The women had been sampling the snacks from time to time, and one or the other had mentioned how tasty everything was.

A bathroom break was called for when the second hour was up. Denise sighed in relief. Her cards weren't improving; if anything, they'd gotten worse. The women reconvened and Barbara Miller suggested they extend their break, to which all agreed.

"What's the latest on Arrow?" Carol asked Denise.

"Fuckin' Arrow!" Denise spat.

"Whoa!" Joan reared back.

"Sorry—" Denise shrugged, "my French ears don't seem to mind my language."

"Oh?" Carol looked her way. "What's the difference between French ears and English ones?"

"Some words don't sound as bad in French."

"Ah-ha," Carol chirped. "Well, tell us about fuckin' Arrow, then."

The other women laughed.

Denise let out a sigh. "There's nothing new. Tom's in Toronto meeting with our banker. But it doesn't look good."

"*Geesh!*" Barbara piped in. "And we all thought the toy industry was a fun business."

"Yeah. Some fun." Denise made a dour face. "If things get any worse Tom and I will have to sell this house and move in with one of you."

"That bad?" Joan asked.

"Yes, unfortunately." Denise managed a wan smile. "But I'm kidding about the moving-in-with-one-of-you part."

* * *

"This is fantastic," Barbara Miller exclaimed fifteen minutes later as she sampled the blue cheese and pear tartelette.

"Not as good as this olive tapenade," Joan insisted.

"Or this baba ghanoush," Carol raved. "You'll have to give me the recipe."

Denise was pleased. She stood and refilled everyone's wine glass. "I meant to ask the three of you about Debbie Stafford. Does anyone know what happened, exactly?"

"All rumors," Barbara said.

Then all three began speaking at once.

"It was self-inflicted."

"No. I hear it was attempted murder."

"I think she was planning her own demise."

"Or someone else was."

"Surely not her husband?"

"Could've been."

Denise was finding it difficult to keep up. "Hold on. I need you guys to slow down."

The girls began apologizing over one another.

Denise waved her hands for silence and they quieted. She asked, "Does anyone know if Debbie is allowed visitors?"

"I believe so," Joan said. "I can check with the hospital and let you know."

"Please do," Denise implored. "Why don't the four of us plan on seeing her together?"

"Good idea," Carol said. And the other women nodded their agreement.

Barbara turned to Denise. "How much longer will Tom be away?"

"He's back on Thursday."

"Would you like to stay with Bill and me?" Barbara offered. "We'd love to have you."

"Why?"

"Because of the murders," Barbara contended. "With Tom out of town, you shouldn't be alone."

Denise seemed to have a moment of reflection, then casually replied, "I'm not worried."

24

February 28

I was more at peace with myself after my trip to Chicago. On the drive home I'd had a good deal of time to reflect, I was determined to resolve the issues foremost on my mind; priority one being Sara. I cared about her and wanted to get to the bottom of what I'd done that upset her the night I slept over. Priority two was my working relationship with Hank Broderick. Unless I found a way to iron out the differences between us, the murder investigation would suffer, and that was something I couldn't afford to let happen.

However, my good intentions where Broderick was concerned already faced a major obstacle. Weeks ago, at his behest, I began interviewing various servicemen who worked at Bonita Palms. Men that he had preselected for me, not as suspects but possible witnesses.

For instance, Gino Scapillati, the fifty-year-old service director with Excalibur Service, who spent twenty percent of his time at the Palms and eighty percent in neighboring communities such as Shadow Wood, Highland Woods, and Spanish Wells. And Fran Bailey, a forty-five-year-old technician with Broad Connections, in the business of solving computer problems, be they Mac or PC.

The list continued, from Manuel Garcia, gardener, to Cecil Rowe, pool specialist. All the men had come in voluntarily and none had seen anything suspicious or the least bit out of the ordinary.

I remembered all of them. And they were back. Each and every one. Broderick had ordered me to conduct this second round of interviews, and it irked the hell out of me. It was all to saddle me with grunt work; bog me down with minutia—keep me out of the way—out of the real investigation so that Broderick could take all the credit should an *actual* lead be uncovered.

I continued with the interviews, but my heart wasn't in it. At noon I headed out of the building to take a long lunch.

* * *

I returned at 2:00 PM to find another group of familiar workers lined up outside my office. I confronted Broderick a few doors down and let him know I was on to his game.

"What're you talking about?" he feigned innocence.

"Give me a break! I interviewed every one of those men a few weeks ago!"

"So?" he said, unable to hide a grin. "I'm just trying to be thorough."

"You're wasting my time, damnit. These men don't know anything. Yet, you dragged them in here *twice*. For what?"

"I told you." His expression turned smug. "We have to be meticulous. Leave nothing to chance."

"And we accomplish that, how?

"By doing what you're doing."

"Bullshit, Hank. Find another grunt," I said, then spun on my heels, exited his office and headed home.

25

March 1

Frank Sinclair was in the bathroom, splashing a dozen drops of Shen Min, a topical hair rejuvenate, on a hardly noticeable bald spot in the back of his head. He'd been using a mirror and the area of thinning hair caught his eye, reminding him that he was in decline. He'd seen it with friends. First the hair, followed by their eyesight, then everything else; an inevitable skid that was irreversible.

The doorbell rang and Frank went to answer it.

"Please sign here," he was instructed by the uniformed FedEx driver.

Though puzzled, he signed, accepted the slim package, and closed the door. He received little mail and something arriving by courier was highly unusual. Frank looked at the shipping label and read who it was from. He wasn't familiar with the sender's name or address and had an inkling they were bogus. With curiosity peaked, he ripped the tab at the top of the sleeve and removed an eight-by-ten envelope.

He undid the clasp. The pictures were in living color and rather explicit. They'd been photoshopped so that the other participants' faces were not in focus—only Frank's. In one close-up: an identifiable mole on Frank's right buttock, next to the penis penetrating him, was very much in high definition. Frank was abhorred. He swore and tried to tear the photographs in one batch but could barely manage a few at a time. He went at it again, until each was in small pieces.

Despite the pixilation, he recognized her body: Melanie, the Barbara Miller lookalike he'd met at his private club. Noncommittal sex was all he'd been after. And he thought it was there for the taking, until he was drugged, then compromised. He vaguely remembered the clicking of a camera.

* * *

Frank found the note in a separate #10 envelope, addressed to George, the fake name he'd used at the club.

THE ENCLOSED PICTURES ARE DUPLICATE COPIES. UNLESS WE RECEIVE $100,000 IN CASH, THEY WILL GO VIRAL. YOU HAVE UNTIL NOON FRIDAY TO COMPLY. CONTACTING THE AUTHORITIES WILL IMMEDIATELY NEGATE THIS OFFER. YOU WILL BE ADVISED BY COURIER WITHIN 24 HOURS AS TO THE LOCATION OF THE DROP. MAY WE SUGGEST THAT IT BEHOOVES YOU…

Behooves? Frank repeated in his head, and he stopped reading. "God almighty!" He didn't believe in coincidences. The only person he knew who used this practically archaic word was Barbara Miller.

Could she be behind this? What would she hope to gain? Does she need money this badly? Or is there a more diabolical reason motivating her?

He continued reading: ...TO NOT DEVIATE FROM OUR INSTRUCTIONS. OTHERWISE, YOU WILL FACE DIRE CONSEQUENCES. WE TRUST YOUR DECISION WILL BE GUIDED BY PRUDENCE.

Frank sucked in his breath. Barbara knew him well, knew that any suggestion of his being gay, or at least depicted in a homosexual sex act, would be a major humiliation and put an end to any chance of maintaining relationships with his female friends and probably most of his buddies.

This woman helped her—Melanie—or whatever the hell her real name is, Frank conjectured. *So now they'll both have to be taken down.* Four days left until Friday; no time to lose.

Frank hurried into his bedroom, removed the .38 Smith & Wesson he kept in a box in his bedroom bureau, and shoved it into his pants pocket. Minutes later he was behind the wheel of his six-series BMW, convertible top left up. He hadn't changed clothes, still dressed in jeans and an old tee shirt with the Miami Dolphins logo on the front.

The drive on 41 heading south took 25 minutes. To get his bearings, Frank first approached his private club. He hadn't been exactly sober when he followed Melanie to her home, but certain landmarks started looking familiar. He knew it was near Pelican Bay. Any house that didn't have a circular driveway and a FOR SALE sign out front was discounted. Frank remembered to look for an oversized wood door with panels of stained glass.

Ten minutes later he saw it: the exclusive-looking bungalow on a street corner, with an air of privilege.

Frank screeched to a stop, got out of the car and rang the

bell like a madman. No one answered. After three more tries he returned to the Beemer, moved to the other side of the street, and set up watch. The noon hour came and went. He second guessed himself, wondering if going to the police was the answer. Let the authorities handle the extortion attempt. But if they didn't make an arrest before Friday he'd be exposed. *Dare I take that chance?*

He was debating his options when a silver Lincoln Continental pulled into the driveway and a middle-aged couple disembarked. Each opened the back door on their side and removed a carry-on with wheels. Frank rocketed out of his car and dashed across the street.

The man was close to his age; corpulent with thinning brown hair. He wore an off-white sport shirt and gray slacks. "Can I help you?" he asked, unnerved by the agitated stranger rapidly approaching.

"Yes. I'm looking for Melanie."

"Melanie?" The man's confusion appeared genuine.

"Are you sure you have the correct address?" the woman asked. She had on a pink cotton dress. She was similar in age to the man, in her mid-fifties. Not quite as overweight, she wore little makeup, yet her skin radiated.

"Yes, I'm sure," Frank said, wanting to be more forceful but not let on that he'd actually been inside. "This was the address she gave me."

"You poor dear. She must have misled you," the woman said kindly, then indicated the man standing beside her. "My husband and I have lived in this house for over twenty years—built it from the ground up. It's for sale, if you're looking for a good buy. But there's no Melanie here, I'm sorry to say."

Frank didn't doubt her sincerity as he looked from her to her husband. Unless they were Oscar-caliber actors, it was unlikely they were in on the scheme. Still, no harm in asking: "Would you happen to know a Barbara Miller?"

The woman's face showed no recognition. "No. Who is she?"

"A close friend of Melanie's."

"Sorry. We don't know her either."

Frank pieced it together: the couple had just returned from a trip. With their house up for sale, it would've been easy for Barbara to obtain the listing, then use the property for her private purpose, as she'd done so often for their assignations. Then, with her partners in crime, set him up for a fall.

"I apologize for having barged in on you like this," he said and turned to go.

"I'm sorry we couldn't be of more help," the woman called after him.

26

March 2

In front of the television, can of Diet Coke in one hand, other hand tapping a thoughtless pattern on my knee. A Florida Everblades hockey game was on but I was oblivious to the TV screen. Dinner had been a ham and Swiss on rye; I hardly remembered eating it.

Can't let Hank's snowballing continue, I told myself. His bringing in those contractors for a second interview was a charade, a mockery of what good police work is all about. Worse, it was turning me into a culpable participant. I had to find a way to stop him. *Ask Sara for advice,* I considered. She's the person I felt I could trust the most.

I glanced at the cordless phone seated in its cradle on a side table. My hand reached out, then withdrew. *Do it!* I punched in the number I knew by heart. After the fifth ring voicemail kicked in and I left a message asking her to call me.

* * *

The following morning I came into work, walked past the area where the deputies and other employees sat, went through the door leading to reception, and stopped short in surprise. Every chair, every inch of floor space, was occupied. Over forty men, sitting or standing, all of whom I'd interviewed before. Their chatter ceased as soon as they noticed me. Their faces turned my way in anticipation.

I already had their names and contact information. "You're all dismissed," I announced. "Sorry if you were inconvenienced." It felt good doing the right thing for a change.

* * *

It didn't take long for Broderick to get wind of what I'd done. I worked on verifying alibis all morning, then went out for lunch. When I returned, he called me into what was once my office and now his.

Mayor Hillier, sitting next to him, leapt to his feet and hollered at me. "You've set us back weeks, maybe months!"

"What the hell were you thinking?" Mayor Torbram, also present, chimed in. "You've obstructed this investigation!"

"Really?" I said casually.

"You willfully ignored a direct order from Hank to conduct interviews," Hillier practically screamed.

"Been there, done that." I shrugged.

"You sonofabitch!" Spittle flew from Mayor Hillier's mouth. "This is grounds for insubordination!"

"Insubordination?" I echoed. "What is this—the army?" I chuckled just to rankle him. "What're ya gonna do? Court-martial me?"

"No. I'm relieving you of your duty," Hillier said with immense satisfaction on his face. "Leave your badge and gun on the desk."

I looked from one to the other. "Your call, but I promise you, gentlemen—this is one decision you'll come to regret."

* * *

I arrived home, knowing it was a matter of time. Hank Broderick didn't have the smarts to solve this case. I could already envision the mistakes he was going to make. Unless he caught an incredible break, the killer would outmaneuver him every step of the way.

I noticed my cordless phone blinking; punched in the code and listened.

"Hi, it's Sara. I got your message. Funny, because I'd been meaning to reach out to you; invite you to dinner at my place tomorrow night. Let me know if you can make it. Bye."

I wondered if the invitation was a peace offering, or if there was something else on her mind.

I reached Sara at her office and asked if I could bring anything.

"Only yourself … and a thick skin."

"Huh? What does that mean?"

"Be prepared to talk."

* * *

I picked up a bottle of *Pouilly Fuissé*. The wine had made an impression the last time I'd been invited to her house and I was hoping to stack the odds in my favor.

Sara accepted the bottle with a brief thank you.

I followed her into the great room. The widescreen TV was on but the sound had been muted.

Sara's blonde hair was pinned up. Her belted burgundy dress fell above her knees. Instead of shoes she was wearing slippers.

"Here—" she proffered a can of Diet Coke and a glass with ice.

I took both from her.

"Make yourself comfortable." She pointed to the couch. "I'll be right back."

I watched her go and took a seat as instructed.

Sara returned with a glass of wine and sat down next to me. When she asked about work, I hesitated.

"Miles?"

"What work?"

"Meaning?"

"I was shit-canned by Hillier. I'm still waiting to hear from Sheriff Norman. He's going to have to get back in the game, whether he likes it or not."

"What happened, exactly?"

I explained how Hank Broderick had me doing multiple b.s. interviews.

"What are you going to do, Miles?"

I shrugged nonchalantly. "Enough about me. What did you want to talk about?"

Sara took a gulp of wine. "The last time you were here you scared the hell out of me."

I stiffened. "What … What did I do?"

Sara looked at me long and hard. She appeared to get it—that I wasn't playing innocent. I really didn't know.

"I came into your bedroom during the night," she said. "I didn't want to be alone. You were asleep. At least, it looked like you were asleep. I slipped into bed and put my arm around you. I wanted to cuddle. And then … you attacked me. You refused to back off no matter how much I protested. It was as if you were … possessed. Finally, I slapped you a good one, then hurried to my own room and locked the door."

Good God! Why can't I remember this? I'd never want to hurt Sara. I recalled the other incident in my recent past. The vivid "dream" when I woke in the morning with bruises on my hands and chest. *What's going on? What's happening to me?*

"Sara, I wish I could explain, but…" Out of the corner of my eye I caught a breaking news flash on the television screen. Sara was aware of it too and she un-muted the sound.

Photographs of the three murder victims were displayed and the male newscaster said, "An arrest just took place in the murders of Cathy Sinclair, Cynthia Gladstone and Jill Derbyshire."

"Huh?" I couldn't believe what I was hearing.

"…acting Deputy Sheriff Hank Broderick announced a few minutes ago that the alleged suspect—"

The screen dissolved for a second and the photographs of the women were replaced by one of a young African American.

I shot up from the couch. "No!"

"Who is he?" Sara asked.

"—is being formally charged with all three murders," the broadcaster continued.

"This is such crap!" I growled. "This kid is innocent. He didn't do it. I know him."

"Miles, who is he?" Sara repeated, just as the announcer said, "Martin Williams, a resident of Bonita Springs, will be arraigned in the morning…"

"The boy's been studying at FIU in Miami for a degree in

business administration," I explained. "His longtime girlfriend left him for another guy. He's been on a sabbatical for the past few months, backpacking in the Florida Panhandle. His parents have a home in Bonita Palms; he visits them from time to time. I know the family well. They were next-door neighbors to the Sinclair's and were one of my first interviews."

"So why was Williams arrested?"

"This is Hank Broderick, Sara. Having a suspect in custody is a desperate attempt to make himself look good. And it's all going to come back to bite him in the ass."

27

March 5

Bill Miller was in pain; seated behind the desk in his home office, file folder open, contemplating the information in front of him. The throbbing ache in his gut made it difficult to concentrate. His cancer was indeed back with a vengeance. He placed another Celenome pill in his mouth, washed it down with water, and waited.

For all intents and purposes his life had ended a few years ago. Bill believed he should have left this earth the minute the clock ticked over on the twenty-fourth hour of the twelfth month of his sixty-ninth year.

But he drew satisfaction from the knowledge that when his financial scam was exposed, it'd be after his demise. And then it wouldn't matter ... to him.

Robbing Peter to pay Paul could only have gone on for so long. Although, when he'd first conceived of the idea, he didn't think it would end this soon. Commodity prices were supposed to fluctuate. Who knew that the U.S. dollar would remain stable for this long, especially in light of the drop in the price of oil? Or that it would strengthen against most of the world's currencies?

Bill had guessed wrong. So now his clients—many of them friends and neighbors —would take the fall. But, if all went as planned, he'd be deceased and Barbara would be the one they'd blame.

He took hold of the contents of the file and read through each of the documents. The forged signature he'd meticulously practiced for over a year looked genuine, with Barbara's replacing his own. He felt confident that even forensic accountants wouldn't be able to uncover the truth.

Soon, his craving for revenge would be assuaged. Some common household appliance to the back of his wife's head would be the easy part. He'd feel no compunction about doing it. And he'd derive infinite pleasure in the leaking out of her cheating brain. The more difficult component would be planting the evidence and throwing the sheriff's department off the scent; make them believe the Bonita Palms' serial killer has struck again.

Talk in the neighborhood was about the arrest of Martin Williams. Bill believed, as did almost everyone else he talked to, that the boy was innocent. To help push Martin's vindication along, Bill thought it a stroke of genius to get rid of Barbara now, while he had the chance. A killing of two birds with one stone. The kid would be exonerated, but most important, his wife would be dead. He couldn't think of anything more satisfying.

*　*　*

June Adams' arms enveloped Barbara Miller, putting her in a rapturous state. *What just happened?* Barbara wondered. She was drenched in sweat, and it felt good, like the best damn workout of her life. Words couldn't describe the multiple sensations that had coursed through her body. June's tongue, an instrument of such dexterity—harsh yet delicate, smooth yet coarse—had coaxed a reaction from nerve endings where none seemed to exist before. Not solely June's tongue but her mouth. Teasing her vagina, then fully appropriating it, until Barbara could stand it no longer. She reached a whole other level; her body thrown into spasms of pleasure and bringing her to tears.

"You did it," she whispered to the assistant golf pro.

"Did what?"

She grew embarrassed.

"Barb?"

"You'll laugh if I tell you."

"No, I won't."

"Took me somewhere I've never gone before."

June smiled to herself, then slowly changed positions, half leaning on an elbow, allowing one of her breasts to nudge Barbara's lips.

It was a temptation Barbara couldn't let pass. She immediately thrust out her tongue and licked. Before long, her mouth encompassed the entire nipple and she began to suck. She reached between June's legs and simultaneously stroked her clitoris. Gently at first, until she worked it into a pattern of sucking and stroking.

June moaned, then shrieked, a prolonged sound most likely heard by the neighbors.

Still, Barbara didn't stop.

"P..l..ea..se," June stammered, going into convulsions.

Barbara continued for a moment longer before releasing her hand.

"My God, my God, my God," June muttered. "I can't get enough of you. Do you know that? I really can't get enough!"

*　*　*

Barbara couldn't say how long she and June slept. All she knew was that the king-size bed was comfortable, and she was exhausted. But it wasn't the kind of fatigue one complained about.

The house she was using today—a bungalow in the community of Grey Oaks—was on the market for 4.6 million dollars. Barbara had gotten the listing last week. The owners lived in England for part of the year and were currently on a cruise in the Orient.

Barbara realized how fortunate she was, to be in her chosen profession. To have the pick of the litter, so to speak, able to use some of the nicest homes for her trysts; with no one being the wiser.

Well, almost no one.

The last time she and June were together she'd arrived home in a blissful state only to find the mirror in her bathroom had been shattered. Beneath it, lying on the carpeted floor, were fragments in unique shades of blue and pink that plainly came from the Venus de Milo statue she'd cherished. Valued at thirty thousand dollars, now gone.

No one had to tell Barbara who was responsible. She'd recently noticed Bill following her in his car. It paralleled his acting more hostile toward her. Nothing was mentioned but deciphering the message was easy.

Now, as June stirred beside her, Barbara blanked out her thoughts.

"Did I fall asleep?" June asked hazily.

"Yes, we both did."

"What time is it?"

Barbara reached over to the nightstand and checked the clock. "Almost noon."

"Oh, my God! I've got to be at work." The covers were flung aside, and June sprang out of bed.

Barbara took delight in watching her. No doubt their age difference—June thirty-one, she forty-nine—added to the allure, helped all the more by June's near-perfect body.

She heard the shower come on and was tempted to join her, to have one last go of it. But her better judgment held her back. *Mustn't overdo a good thing*, she reminded herself.

June came out of the bathroom. Barbara got out of bed and approached. She gave her a hug and kissed her goodbye. She watched June leave, already missing her touch.

* * *

Barbara was humming to herself when she walked into the house. "Hello," she called. "I'm home."

No answer.

The door to Bill's office was closed. She knocked and waited. No response.

"Bill?" she raised her voice.

"What the hell do you want?" came his reply through the locked door.

There was a meanness in his voice that Barbara had gotten used to. "I said, I'm home."

"Bully for you."

"Can I get you anything?"

He didn't reply.

"Bill?"

"What?"

"I asked if I can get you something."

"No. Go away—I'm busy."

"Oh, I'm sorry. How are you feeling?"

"Just ... peachy keen."

"Honestly?"

"For fuck's sake! Can you not take a hint and leave me alone?"

Barbara half expected the rebuke, but it still stung. She backed away and went to the master bedroom.

* * *

The room was large—20' x 30'. She and Bill each had a sitting area and a private safe built into the wall on either side of the bed. Both kept personal possessions locked inside.

She glanced at the Picasso print concealing the safe behind it. The contents now included the original thumb drive and a copy of the letter she'd sent to Frank Sinclair. She was owed a favor by an old acquaintance, Patricia Greer, alias "Melanie". Patricia headed an escort service and her place of operation—her private home—was once raided by the police. Barbara had sold Patricia the property and had been able to reassign the ownership documents to an offshore corporation so that it couldn't be seized in the ensuing investigation. Thus, it was a matter of calling in a favor. After explaining her predicament, Patricia readily agreed to help target Frank Sinclair.

Barbara would've given anything to have been there when he

received the package. The look on his face would've made her day ten times over.

I'll teach the bastard to ignore me! To use me for more than a year and then dump me like I'm some toy he's bored with! Barbara may have acted like she wasn't bothered by it, but she damn well was. *No one does this to me and gets away with it. I'm the one who decides when an affair is over. I'm the one in control. Always was and always will be. And now the sonofabitch will pay!*

28

March 12

I sat on my couch thinking about the arrest of Martin Williams. It was plainly a mistake that eventually would be uncovered. Meanwhile, Sheriff Norman had been coasting toward his retirement, but with "trusty" Hank failing badly with his perp for the murders, the sheriff would have to soon recognize he'd best step up to the plate.

Lunch hour came and went, then someone rang my doorbell. I hadn't bothered to shower or shave for the better part of a week and was dressed in an old pair of sweats, so I was reluctant to answer it. When the person began to knock, I figured, *What the hell.*

Sara Churchill—as attractive as ever despite the frown creasing her brow—waited to be invited in.

I stepped aside to give her room.

"You didn't reply to my voicemails," she said, sounding miffed, brushing past me into the vestibule.

"What voicemails?" I said, immediately regretting the lie.

"Only five or six of them. What's the matter with you?"

I gave my patented shrug.

"I was worried about you, Miles. I thought something had happened to you."

"I'm sorry. It's just—" It was ironic to find our roles reversed. I'd been the one who desperately wanted to continue our relationship. Yet, knowing what I knew now, that I'd manhandled her with no memory of having done so, made me reluctant to be anywhere near her.

"Is it because of what I told you?" Sara asked, making the correct assumption. "Because if it is, I'm sorry. I never should've said anything. I ... could've been wrong. Maybe I misinterpreted your intentions."

I saw what she was doing, trying to mitigate my burden of guilt. "You scared the hell out of me," I confessed. "If what you said is true—and I don't doubt you for a minute—then something weird is happening to me. I need to ... find out what's going on."

"What *is* going on?" Sara echoed with caution.

"I—I don't know. But it's obvious I can't be trusted."

"Miles—"

"Look," I gathered myself, then took the plunge: "you're the only woman I want to be with, Sara. You make me feel special. I very much want to continue seeing you. But you'll have to be patient. Let me get to the bottom of my problem."

"What problem, Miles?" Sara said in exasperation.

I sighed. "I don't know what it is. *That's* the problem. All I know is that I have lapses in memory during which I do things I can't explain. Please bear with me. I need time to figure it out."

She headed for the door, then turned. "Better not take too long, Miles."

* * *

"Sheriff?" Brad Pedersen barked out tentatively, less than an hour after Sara had left.

Two callers in the same afternoon? Why am I suddenly so popular? I opened the door and said, "I was never sheriff. Simply deputy sheriff. And in case I need to remind you, I'm no longer in that position."

"You still are to me, sir. Always will be."

"Your loyalty is misplaced. Anyway, what are you doing here?"

"I need to tell you something."

I led the way into the kitchen where I invited Pedersen to have a seat. "Still take it black?" I asked, indicating the Keurig machine next to the stove.

"Yes, I do."

The sergeant accepted the coffee, then turned serious. "There's been another murder, sir. Last night. During the supper hour."

My heart jumped. "Who was it?"

"Barbara Miller."

"My God!" It took me a moment to compose myself. "Same M.O. as the others?"

"Not quite. A knife was used."

"A knife?"

"Yes. But all other aspects match the previous murders—no forced entry, same time of day, murder weapon belonging to the deceased and left at the scene.

"And the Williams kid is still in jail?"

"Yes, he is."

"Hmm. Are you thinking what I'm thinking, Brad?"

"I am, sir. That's the reason I'm here."

29

March 14

Larry Stafford was alone having a late lunch in the Bonita Palms clubhouse after completing a round of golf. He'd never had the money or the inclination for the sport when he was growing up. But once he'd entered university he was swayed by his friends to give it a try, and it had evolved from there. The fact that he was merely an average player never bothered him.

Larry was by himself because the other members of his foursome had prior commitments. He didn't mind, however. It felt good occasionally to not have to make conversation.

The clubhouse had recently been renovated at a cost of hundreds of thousands of dollars. He took in the vaulted ceiling, the excess wainscoting, and the rosewood dining tables set in various configurations, seating from two to ten. There was an abundance of mahogany, and more television sets, in more size configurations—all located in the bar area—than was necessary. Quite a room, for those who could afford to belong to the club.

Such is the prerequisite of a successful golf community, Larry mused to himself. If you got it, flaunt it. Not just a mantra of the nouveau riche, he knew.

He sipped his iced tea and tried to while away the time by observing the other club members, few of whom were alone. The majority seemed relaxed and in good spirits, enjoying themselves.

Larry wished he and his wife could enjoy themselves even half as much. The last month had been one of the worst of his life. He'd spent most of his time at the hospital. The prognosis had remained up in the air, especially at the beginning, and he thought for sure he would lose her.

No one knew exactly what had happened. Debbie was too weak to shed any light on her condition and the doctors couldn't figure it out, at least not until they discovered what pills she had ingested. The overdose could have killed her.

Her recovery had gone smoothly from that point onwards. One minute, Larry was having to consider making funeral arrangements, the next he was filled with hope. As his wife's strength improved so did her mindset. By the time he brought her home two weeks ago Debbie had renewed energy.

But before long she reverted to her old self. The weight she'd lost during her hospitalization was back, her religious fervor had re-intensified, and her attitude toward him became even more confrontational.

Enough, Larry told himself. It was too painful to dwell upon his situation. He glanced at his watch: 3:05 p.m.

He signed his lunch chit and left. Once in his car he didn't have to think about his destination. He'd been following the same routine for a while. Golf or a movie; often a combination of both, all timed perfectly to get him home no earlier than eight-thirty in the evening. By then his wife would invariably be out of it and too tired to start another argument.

30

March 15.

BONITA PALMS KILLER STRIKES AGAIN!
COMMUNITY IS TERRIFIED!
ACTING DEPUTY SHERIFF BRODERICK ASKED TO RESIGN!
SUSPECT MARTIN WILLIAMS RELEASED FROM CUSTODY!

* * *

The call came soon afterwards. "I need to see you," Sheriff Norman said.

I wasn't surprised to hear from him. "Welcome back to the living," I said with no reserve of sarcasm.

"I deserve that," he said after a pause. "Look—I'm hoping you can meet me for lunch."

"When?"

"Today, please. I'm sure you've been following the news. We need to talk."

"Today's fine."

"Okay then," he said, the relief in his voice unmistakable. "How about the coffee shop at the Hyatt off 41? It's kind of isolated. We can have some privacy there."

"Sure. What time?"

"How is one o'clock?"

"One is good."

* * *

The sheriff was already there when I arrived, attired in his dress uniform, so crease-free it appeared to have been ironed less than a minute ago. He stood from the table and thrust out his hand. We shook and took our seats. The strain Sheriff Norman was feeling showed. His thick brown hair was still styled in waves, blue/green eyes penetrating as always. But his easy smile was absent and the haggard look on his face suggested a serious lack of sleep. The man was sixty-five but looked ten years older.

"I'm truly sorry," he said. "I should've stayed more involved."

I waved it off. "No apology necessary. If I was zeroing in on retirement, I'd probably have done the same as you."

"I doubt it," the sheriff conceded. "Meanwhile, Hillier had the authority to act on my behalf but only up to a certain point. He overstepped his bounds when he fired you. I should have told him he was out of line. But the case had stalled. I thought Hank, being fresh blood, could jumpstart it. Guess you knew him better than I did. Anyway…"

"Ready to order, gentlemen?" the waitress broke in.

Sheriff Norman asked for the crab cakes and I told her I'd have the same.

"I want you back," he said once she was gone. "I can assure you there'll be no further interference. Not from Mayor Hillier, nor Mayor Torbram. I'm sure you know I released Broderick, so he's out of the picture. This'll be your investigation to run, with complete autonomy and my full backing." He removed an envelope from his inside jacket pocket and handed it to me.

I opened it and read that I was being rehired with a salary bump of ten percent. I was surprised at the generous offer, but not by the news of Broderick's demise. I'd known his days were numbered right from the get-go. I'd sized the man up as pure ego the moment I met him. Arresting Martin Williams just to make himself look good proved my point.

"No one gets this kind of increase," the sheriff said. "And my replacement will have to live with it. Speaking of which, I know *you* have no interest in running for my job.

"Well, sir," I said, "that's a correct assumption." And we both had a good laugh.

"So?"

"All right," I said softly, "let's put this killer behind bars."

* * *

I phoned Sara and gave her the news.

"This calls for a celebration … like, dinner tonight at my house," she proclaimed.

I hesitated. "Not a good idea."

"Why not?"

"We talked about this, Sara. I still don't trust myself."

"Well, let's make it lunch, then," she insisted. "But it might have to wait for a little over a week. I'm jammed at work and there's a conference in Atlanta I need to attend in-between."

I smiled to myself. "Lunch will be fine. And thank you for understanding."

I knew this would be my last opportunity for a long while to relax. I spent the rest of the afternoon with the latest novel by David Baldacci. Then I barbecued a steak for dinner, aiming to spoil myself a bit. Afterwards I listened to Harry Connick, Jr. on my iPod, keeping my eyes closed and willing myself to zone out.

It was early, not yet 9:00 PM, when I went into the bathroom for a couple of Narvia pills, before returning to the couch.

* * *

I awoke with a start, sprawled out on the carpet and still fully dressed. But my shirt had several buttons popped off and was badly torn.

I could hear the television but didn't remember turning it on. I tried sitting up. My head was pounding so I lay back down. I reviewed the events of the day: lunch with the sheriff, calling Sara, reading a book, dinner, Harry Connick, Jr. ... *What else had I done?*

31

Earlier the same week

It was still fresh in your mind, the blade entering Barbara Miller's body, tearing through cartilage and tissue, the shock on Barbara's face adding immeasurably to the satisfying thrill of it all.

She had been effusive when she'd opened the door to her house by way of invitation and announced her husband was out and not expected home for hours. She was dressed as provocatively as ever: red shorts that were too short, and so tight the indent of her crotch was evident. Pink blouse unbuttoned practically to her navel, exposed bosom unencumbered by a bra.

"Come in," she'd said with a welcoming smile. "I have beer in the fridge, white wine in the cooler, scotch, bourbon and Canadian whisky in the bar. What's your pleasure?"

Your reply was automatic: "Water with ice, please. I was in the neighborhood. Just thought I'd drop in to say hello."

"Really?" Barbara said, eyes dancing. "Isn't that nice. Follow me…"

She headed to the kitchen and you followed. It took concentration not to act impulsively, your eyes flicking this way and that, searching for something—anything—that could be used as a weapon.

Nothing seemed appropriate. There were decorative pieces on pedestals, either too big and clumsy or no bulk to them at all. This had never happened before. Tightened nerve ends threatened your control, but giving up was out of the question. And then...

The knife-block—dark wood with eight inviting handles—SANTOKU STAINLESS STEEL in capital letters—resting on the granite countertop. But you'd never used a knife before so the search continued, roaming every which way until the realization hit that nothing else would work.

Barbara turned her back and it was now or never; reaching out, you snatched the closest one, with a six-and-a-half-inch blade.

At the fridge, Barbara was gathering ice cubes into a bucket. You stepped up behind her, knife raised, when Barbara unexpectedly glanced over her shoulder. She screamed, whirled around, and threw the ice bucket at you.

You batted it away with one arm. Didn't feel a thing. So focused were you on your mission.

"Please ... don't!" Barbara pleaded. "I'll do anything you ask."

You lowered the knife with a look of compassion.

The ruse worked. Barbara saw this as remorse and capitulation. She raised her left hand, placed her right hand over her heart. "I swear I won't tell anyone. This'll be our secret."

You nodded in agreement. Barbara let out a sigh of relief. And that's when you jabbed the knife into her upper chest, just below the clavicle.

"W…Why?" Barbara barely managed.

The next plunge went deep into her stomach, carrying with it as much force as possible.

Barbara's scream died as she collapsed on the floor. She was bleeding out. You steered clear of the pooling blood to avoid leaving footprints, then slashed her breasts, back and forth, again and again.

32

March 18

It was good to be back at work. Things were different but in a good way. I sensed it the minute I walked through the door to my office. There was a hum or buzz, an inaudible sound only I could hear, a vibe echoing off the walls, telling me this was where I belonged.

Brad Pedersen was first to greet me. "Sheriff—"

"Deputy sheriff."

"Welcome home." He placed a 24" x 10" x 6" gift-wrapped box on my desk.

I went to open it, but he stopped me. "Hold it. This needs an explanation. Everyone on staff made a contribution. We've been anticipating your return, and we're all glad to have you back."

I picked up the box and noted the heft; about ten pounds at least. "Good speech. May I open it now?"

"Yes, sir."

"Nothing's going to fly out at me, is it?"

"No, sir."

"Stop calling me 'sir'."

"Yes, sir."

I undid the wrapping and peered into the box. Tissue paper enveloped an oblong object. I removed the paper and held up a metallic sculpture of Sylvester Stallone as Rocky, over a foot and a half tall, nine inches wide. "Cool," I said, pleased with the gift.

"Sheriff—"

"Shh," I stopped Pedersen before he could say anything further. "I'm admiring it."

He indicated a new photograph on the corkboard. "I need to bring you up to speed."

I put the statue down. Barbara Miller was the most flagrantly sexual person I'd ever met. Yet there was something about her I couldn't help but like.

"Similar M.O. to the others," Pedersen said. "Husband away from the house. No forced entry."

"Still think it's the same perp?"

"I do. Mrs. Miller was young and strong. The medical examiner believes Miller tried warding off the killer by throwing a bucket of ice at him. She knew whoever this was. She let him into her home. No doubt about it."

I studied the stab wounds in the photograph. "You said the knife was left at the scene?"

"Yes, sir. It was part of a set of eight that belonged to the victim."

"Umm. Very strange. Using a knife to kill someone when he never used one before. It's quite personal, especially the way Mrs. Miller's breasts were slashed after she was dead. I interviewed the husband, Bill. The man was stoic. He was either unable to come to grips with his wife's murder or it didn't bother him in the least.

But his alibi's solid. Tell me, were any slipups found? A morsel of evidence that could help us?"

"No, sir. None whatsoever."

I sighed. Nothing like reality to dampen my mood after a mere few minutes back on the job.

* * *

The Miller house in the Augusta subdivision of Bonita Palms was over five thousand square feet and two stories high. I remembered the interesting circular columns fronting the door—one on each side—rising to the roof.

Bill Miller had given me an extra key and I let myself in. It was still an active crime scene, so Bill was currently staying at a hotel until we were through processing the evidence. My team advised Bill that they'd let him know when he could return.

The doorbell rang and I went to answer it.

"Sheriff Delany?" The man was average height, middle-aged, with close-cropped red hair and an Irish accent.

"That's me. You must be the locksmith."

"I am, sir." He handed me his business card. "Sean Fitzgerald, at your service."

We shook hands and I led the way into the master bedroom.

It was spacious, with deep-pile carpet, but a good example of money gone to waste, starting with the fireplace—something not quite practical for Florida—to the oversized television set that was too big for the room, to the outlandish mirror recessed into the ceiling.

I approached Barbara Miller's side of the bed and pointed to the Picasso print. "The safe is behind the painting."

"Combination still a mystery?" the locksmith asked for verification.

I nodded. "Even the deceased's husband doesn't know it." In fact, Bill was curious himself about what was in the safe. Barbara constantly refused his inquiries and now that she was dead, he was pleased not to wait any longer. I'd no sooner made the request when he scribbled out written permission to crack the safe, provided I divulge to him what I found inside. I agreed but with the restriction that any evidence that might implicate Barbara in a crime, by point of law, would have to be sealed, pending an investigation.

Fitzgerald placed the black case he was carrying, which resembled a narrow tool box, on the bed. "I'll need your signature, Sheriff."

I reviewed the legal document he handed me, which more or less protected his butt, then signed in the appropriate place.

The locksmith went to work. I'd expected him to take out a stethoscope-like device that would've enabled him to hear the clicking of the tumblers. When I asked, he said I shouldn't believe what I saw on television or in the movies. Instead, he extracted a power drill affixed with a bit that could cut into metal. The noise was deafening.

* * *

It took close to a half-hour and I remained by the locksmith's side throughout. When the door to the safe popped open, Fitzgerald backed away.

I thanked the man for his service, saw him out, and returned to the bedroom. There was far less than I'd anticipated finding:

Barbara Miller's passport, a wallet containing seven hundred dollars in cash, miscellaneous jewelry, and an eight-by-ten manila envelope. I felt foolish. I'd been grasping at straws for so long, I was hoping today would be different and not another waste of time. Then I removed the contents of the envelope ... and everything changed.

There was a thumb drive as well as printed color pictures of Frank Sinclair. Close-ups from every imaginable angle. Frank was either in ecstasy or agony; I couldn't tell which. And my image of him being a macho heterosexual evaporated. I would definitely not be sharing this part of my find with Bill Miller.

I read the letter, addressed to George—which I took to be Frank's alias—and my pulse started to race. Not a waste of time after all; far from it. Something nefarious was going on, and I now had a strong motive for murder: blackmail in its ugliest form.

33

Eight days ago

Move! Frank Sinclair told himself. *Move while there's still time. Before the police come looking for me. Don't bother to pack a suitcase. Throw a few necessities into a carry-on bag and get the hell out of Florida.*

Frank left the house through the garage, piled into his BMW and hit the road. With Barbara Miller now dead, he was sure it was only a matter of time before a police investigation would uncover her blackmail scheme, which would make him the number one suspect in her murder. There was no way he wanted to risk being questioned.

He had a little over $20,000 in cash with him; an emergency fund he kept hidden in the garage, to support his philandering lifestyle. He also had six credit cards in his wallet, but they were useless. Credit cards left a trail and could easily lead the cops to his whereabouts.

The first few hours of the drive were nerve wracking and he didn't know what to do with himself other than pay attention to the road ahead. Then Frank glanced in his rearview mirror and noticed a black van, a vehicle he thought he'd seen before. Perhaps at the last rest stop? Something in his subconscious made the connection. It didn't necessarily mean someone was following him, but Frank needed to be sure.

He'd been traveling below the sixty-five mile per hour speed limit. He now moved into the passing lane and stepped it up to seventy. The van was the fourth car behind. As Frank accelerated so did the van.

He increased his speed to eighty, overtook six other cars, then pulled back into the inside lane and decelerated. The van did the same, matching him speed for speed, maneuver for maneuver, the driver maintaining the four-car spread between them.

The problem with any modern expressway today, Frank realized, was that there was nowhere to hide. He could pull in at the next rest area, or he could take the upcoming exit and see where it led. But what good would it do? If the tail was a professional, he'd never lose him.

Frank understood it wasn't the police; if it was, they would have stopped him long ago. No, if he had to guess, he'd put his money on that girl, Melanie. Well, maybe not her exactly, but one of her friends or associates. It had taken organization to set him up. If she was as close to Barbara as he suspected, then she'd want her murder avenged.

But if someone thought that they could intimidate him, they had another *think* coming. Frank had always been prepared to fight fire with fire; it wasn't in his DNA to turn the other cheek.

Without giving it further thought, he activated his turn signal, eased his foot off the accelerator, and braked hard. As he pulled off to the side, the car slid a little on some loose gravel, but Frank regained control.

He came to a full stop and looked in his rearview mirror, expecting to see the van. Instead, it went sailing past. He tried to catch sight of the driver. The vehicle's tinted windows were too dark, preventing him from being able to see inside.

34

March 21

Early afternoon on a Wednesday and the corkboard was our focal point. Appended were the latest crime-scene photographs. Alongside me were Brad Pedersen, Scott Wellington, and Walter Diggs of the FBI.

Diggs was someone I'd worked with in the past; one of the few Feds I trusted. He was tall, 6'3", wearing a well-fitted dark-gray suit and conservative black tie. I'd invited him to consult with us, figuring it was best to be proactive and get him involved. Otherwise the FBI would likely appoint someone else and I'd be at risk of facing another Hank Broderick situation, working with a guy who'd try to run roughshod over me.

I directed everyone's attention to Barbara Miller's picture on the board. "This is getting far more personal, gentlemen. The use of a knife is something we haven't seen before." I paused. "Brad—anything more on linking Mrs. Miller to Frank Sinclair?"

The sergeant let his frustration show. "Nothing. The woman remains an enigma."

Agent Diggs, comfortable in his area of expertise, approached the corkboard and removed the letter I'd uncovered in the safe at the Miller residence. "Even though this is addressed to someone named George, and despite the fact it's signed by someone named Melanie, we know from the FedEx receipt it had been delivered to Frank Sinclair's home. So, it's safe to assume that George was an alias Mr. Sinclair used when he was out on the prowl. My people are working on that connection. And we'll get there soon. There's no doubt about that."

Spoken like a true feebee, I almost said aloud.

"Meanwhile," the agent continued, "our profilers have carefully gone through the details of each murder. The evidence indicates that our doer is male, older than what you'd normally find—in his fifties or even sixties—well educated, and of an affluent background."

I noted the information, then turned my attention to Scott Wellington. "Where are we on Mr. Miller's alibi?"

"It's rock solid," the corporal said. "The man was getting a haircut at 5th Avenue Barber & Shave in Naples when the murder took place."

"Okay," I said. I was about to call the meeting to an end when Diggs stopped me.

"There's something else about Bill Miller that you need to be aware of. During our interview, the man was reluctant to talk about his business, which peaked our curiosity. We could tell something didn't pass the smell test so we're delving into it. If we get the slightest hint of probable cause, we'll ask a judge for a subpoena."

The news, while related, wasn't a high priority. "Fine then," I said. "Look—let's take a break for now. We all know what we have to do. Let's meet back here tomorrow morning."

* * *

After 7:00 p.m. I still hadn't left my office. I was revisiting reports, hoping to find that seemingly "insignificant" clue every case has that cracks it wide open. But no such luck.

By the time I got home I was hungry and wanted something quick. I picked out a lasagna dinner from the freezer and zapped it in the microwave. While eating I caught up with local events by reading the *Fort Myers News Press*. Dessert was skipped but I made a Keurig coffee and took it with me into the great room.

I turned on the TV, changed channels a few times, finally went to my PVR. The list of unwatched shows and movies was short, but I was able to find something interesting.

Side Effects was released a number of years ago. I'd missed seeing it even though Steven Soderbergh was a director I admired. With a cast that included Jude Law, Rooney Mara, and Catherine Zeta-Jones, I figured it was worth my time.

For once, I wasn't disappointed. The acting was as good as I expected, and the storyline held me intrigued. From the time Rooney Mara smashed her vehicle into the parking garage wall—after first attaching her seatbelt—to her mood swings, prescription drug ingestion, to the murder of her husband, I was hooked.

But the further along the movie played the more an idea began to creep into my head. I couldn't fully define it yet, but it was there, waiting to see the light. Meanwhile, I continued to follow the drama playing out on my television screen. From the woman's psychiatrist taking the fall, to the use of drugs as her potential alibi, to the suspicion that it was all an act and the woman was lying. The ending was worth the wait. The medication played no role whatsoever. Ironically, there were no side effects. The drugs had simply been used as an excuse.

The fact that justice prevailed was a satisfying conclusion. I took hold of the clicker, was about to shut off the TV, when the idea nagging inside my brain became clear, and I froze.

What if—I hypothesized—a particular prescription medication really could cause a neurosis? Really could change people in ways that couldn't be imagined? Really could scramble their sanity and turn them violent?

* * *

Up on my feet, I began to pace, telling myself to calm down. But I was amped, facing a reality that was far too personal. My own medication could've been what led to actions beyond my control: fighting with total strangers, being unconsciously aggressive with a woman I truly cared about. How far a leap would it be to murder?

Four heinous crimes had been committed; none of which made sense. The victims trusted their assailant. There was no forced entry; each allowed him into her home. Whoever he was, the women had no clue that he'd come to do them harm.

I asked myself, *How many people are there in our lives that we put complete trust in?* A spouse would most likely be number one, followed by parents, children, and finally close friends. *Who else?* Doctors, accountants, and … deputy sheriffs?

I continued pacing, believing I might have stumbled upon the cause. But had I also found the number one suspect?

35

Eleven days ago

One down, two to go—like it was preordained, Bill Miller mused. No effort on his part. Nothing he'd had to do. Life taking its course; or in this case, the serial killer simply doing his thing. He only wished he could have been there, a proverbial fly-on-the-wall, watching Barbara die a brutal, agonizing death.

Bill was presently sitting close to Frank Sinclair's house in a black Dodge van. Renting the vehicle had become a necessity. His doctor had filed a compulsory report with the government that prohibited him from driving. Someone in his medical condition, ingesting his profile of drugs, wasn't to be trusted on the road. But Bill was able to purchase a forged driver's license and used it with the rent-a-car company.

The same connection who provided the counterfeit document was also able to supply a handgun with silencer and plant a bug in Frank's car. Bill had met Tommy Anderson in a bar when he'd first arrived in Florida and had kept his information on file. Anderson worked out of a liquor store in downtown Fort

Myers. Bill had used him once before—to strong-arm a client who threatened to expose his financial scheme—so he knew Anderson was trustworthy.

The tracking implement attached to Sinclair's car was cheap, with a radius of one mile. Bill was provided with a monitoring device similar to a small handheld calculator. It served a purpose solely if he remained within range.

Bill planned to follow Frank until an opportunity presented itself—with no other cars in the vicinity as witnesses—and shoot Frank from the open passenger side window of the van, making him look like a victim of road rage. The assistant golf pro, June Adams, was next on his list. She and Frank had consorted with Barbara and both had to pay the price. Bill knew his medical condition was rapidly deteriorating. In fact, his doctor wanted him admitted to hospital. But first he needed to satisfy his craving for revenge.

* * *

His wife's funeral had been held in Buffalo, New York, on a cold, snow-driven day. The Presbyterian church, laden with floral arrangements, was almost filled to capacity with relatives and friends. Barbara had attended here as a child in the neighborhood where she grew up.

The soprano's voice reverberated against the walls, and the lilting melody of Barbara's favorite hymn, *How Great Thou Art*, brought several mourners to tears.

"Please rise," the minister intoned.

Bill had a problem getting to his feet, but he fought his discomfort. The last thing he wanted was to show weakness.

A prayer was recited, and the congregation was asked to be seated once again. What followed was laudatory praise from Barbara's peers with both amusing as well as poignant anecdotes. Next, the minister's review of Barbara's life: the schools she'd attended, her brief career as a nurse, her marriage and eventual move to Florida.

"Wherever she went," the minister read from his notes, "no matter whom she encountered, Barbara Miller left an indelible mark. It says much about her—the way she made us feel good about ourselves."

Yeah, right ... like when she cheated on me? Bill thought bitterly. He brought his attention to his wife's coffin positioned near the alter. He wished he could feel something meaningful instead of the cold emptiness in his heart. He wondered what there was that prevented him from making a clean sweep, to simply admit the error of his ways, to meet his Maker with a clear conscience.

But my conscience is clear. That's the ironic part. I don't feel guilty at all. Frank and June will get what they deserve. If I have to leave this earth under a dark cloud, so be it. I don't even care if it means being cursed to eternal damnation.

* * *

Bill sighed, sat up straighter and peered out the window of the van. His stomach was inflamed. To be expected, he figured, with the cancer spreading and his constant intake of prescription medicines. Pills to slow the disease's progression, pills for the pain, pills to offset the harmful effects of the other pills.

The garage door at Frank's house began to rise finally, and Bill's tracking device came to life with a beep. There was Frank, behind the wheel of his BMW, accelerating away at a surprisingly fast clip.

Bill followed—from the Bonita Palms complex, north on 41, then east on Corkscrew Road. By the time Frank entered Interstate 75 heading north, Bill had fought off his pain and was fully alert.

It was only when Frank passed Sarasota, then Tampa, that he grew concerned. Bill hadn't planned on a trip this long. And he cursed himself for having skimped on a cheap monitor as he'd now have to stay close. No matter what Frank tried, he kept up. When Frank changed to the passing lane, or slowed down and returned to the inside lane, he did the same, always remaining four car-lengths behind.

There were stops for coffee and gas, then the journey continued. Frank's moves soon became a little too deliberate, and Bill knew he was made. Not that it mattered. The minute Frank entered Interstate 24 and headed west, Bill figured out exactly where he was going. For this reason, when the man abruptly pulled onto the shoulder of the road, Bill drove past him.

"See you soon," Bill mouthed aloud. "Much sooner than you think…"

36

March 21
Evening

I forced myself to sit on the couch and wondered how far I should take my newfound theory: the harm a prescription drug was doing to people, including myself.

Cathy Sinclair had been killed at approximately 6:43 p.m. on January 4. I couldn't remember where I was at the time. Was it possible the pill I was taking caused me to have one of my blackouts? Mrs. Sinclair knew me well. She would've invited me into her home without a moment's hesitation.

I moved on the next victim, Cynthia Gladstone, and tried to think back.

Where was I at the time of her homicide? Yes ... Sara Churchill and I were having dinner. If I was blameless for the Gladstone murder, wouldn't I be blameless for the others? Unless... Unless there were more than one perp? Me and someone else?

The Derbyshire and Miller murders also drew a blank. I didn't have a clue where I was or what I'd been doing on either day.

Face it! I warned myself. *This isn't something to be ignored. Even if it ends up implicating me.*

* * *

I was looking down and my attention went to the copies of *Golf Digest, Entertainment Weekly,* and *Time* sitting on my coffee table. I skimmed through the periodicals, searching out the ads I remembered seeing.

Relianz, a pill from the Pritzer company, was used to treat moderate to severe rheumatoid arthritis. The very small print cautioned that taking the medication could lower one's immune system, thereby hurting its ability to fight infections and might also lead to an increased risk of certain cancers, including lymphoma.

I shook my head in disbelief.

Loquis treated blood clots. But for some patients the tablet could result in bleeding from the gums, or heavier than normal menstrual bleeding which, although rather rare, could lead to death.

Bayo, a drug for asthma, carried with it the risk of vomiting, sudden breathing problems, serious allergic reactions, increased blood pressure, a fast or irregular heartbeat, and the possibility of adrenal insufficiency that could get worse or, in extreme cases, even kill you.

I flipped from an advertisement for Leftix, to one for Myloca, each including a warning on possible suicidal thoughts. And finally, one called Delarian, to treat vaginal symptoms of menopause such as dryness, burning, and painful intercourse. The warning suggested that the medicine could cause bloating, stomach cramps, as well as dizziness, mental depression, mood disturbances, dementia…

I closed the final magazine in disgust, having read enough. *Why would anyone dare take these drugs?*

Americans were essentially being poisoned. Women, men, and—I had no doubt—children. Yes, the warnings were there, but how often were they followed? If a doctor prescribed a medication it was human nature for most patients to accept it as being safe. We trust our medical practitioners, and we count on the FDA to safeguard us.

But are we truly being protected?

37

March 23.
Late afternoon

A jagged little pill, bringing back memories of Alanis Morissette. A small orb that you placed on your tongue and swallowed with water. As always, a change occurred, seldom quite the same. Lethargic mind and body at first, then the opposite. Unpredictable. Not easy to comprehend.

Fifteen minutes later a voice began to rattle in your head, it hurt. Each word sounded harsh; clipped and insistent. You were unable to block it out. Fighting it was pointless. It was best to give in, roll with the tide, go with the flow.

Against your will you frowned. The pain increased exponentially with each wrinkle of your forehead. Still, you left the house and got into your car, with no idea where you were going. The vehicle drove as if on its own volition, then it stopped.

You made your way onto the sidewalk. The sun might've been shining. There was heat on your face and upper body, and the warmth felt good. But the feeling didn't last. The throbbing in your skull was unyielding; it took great willpower not to scream.

*　*　*

Joan Ward, wearing a blue pantsuit, was surprised to see you. "Seth is playing golf," she said.

You remained silent.

"To what do I owe the pleasure? Would you like to come in?"

She was already leading the way, so you followed.

"Can I get you a drink?"

You weren't thirsty, but you said you'd appreciate a glass of water with ice.

"Just *water*? Okay. Coming right up."

The urge to do harm was overpowering. You started to follow Joan toward the kitchen, eyes roaming every which way. There was nothing useful in sight. No hammer or knife; not even a pot or pan. You'd been counting on at least the heft of a heavy skillet. You figured there'd be one in the lower cabinets but how would you get to it without arousing suspicion? Confusion reigned. You quickly moved away, ending up in the great room.

"Just be another minute," Joan called from the kitchen. "I'm putting a few hors d'oeuvres together."

About sixty seconds to find a suitable weapon. You began counting to yourself as you stealthily searched the room, reminding yourself that a decision was necessary.

Nothing! you cursed inwardly.

The only option left was to strangle her with your bare hands. It was tempting, but could you do it? You heard Joan's footsteps approaching. Too many variables. Too many things could go wrong. You'd seen enough cop shows on TV to know that touching the victim in any way meant telltale DNA could be left behind.

Time was up. You moved quickly from the great room to the hallway, to the front entrance. You fled the house. Mission aborted.

It didn't dawn on you until you were halfway home that you'd forgotten to close the door behind you.

38

March 24

On Saturday I joined Sara on the lanai at the back of her house. The old-fashioned metal table was set for two. We took a seat on cushioned, wrought-iron chairs. The temperature was comfortable, hovering in the low eighties.

"I missed you," Sara said, looking deep into my eyes.

"I missed you as well."

"How's the investigation going?"

I brought her up to speed, then offered my theory on the possible connection between a prescription drug and criminal behavior.

I expected her to scoff, but Sara grew serious. "My God, I had a cousin who went off the rails after taking Fenox to treat her arthritis. Previously, she'd never done anything unlawful in her life. Then she began shoplifting—cheap items she didn't even need. I agree that what you're saying is a possibility, Miles. This hits close to home."

I hesitated, knowing there was a second part to my theory, something I really wanted to share with her, about the chance of my own culpability. But no matter how I imagined vocalizing it, it always came out wrong. Was I guilty? Could I be satisfying a hidden impulse locked deep inside my psyche, unaware of what I was doing, becoming violent during a drug-induced blackout?

I'd done my research. My Narvia medication was proven to be effective in treating anxiety, but what were the real side effects? Uncovering what those might be was my challenge.

And where will it lead? There was at least one killer out there. I was convinced I was on the right trail. But I needed more solid evidence to prove my theory ... even if it came back and pointed a finger at two killers, one of them being me.

* * *

I asked Sara, "What are we having for lunch?"

"Brunch," she corrected. "What's your preference?"

"I leave it up to you."

She returned about fifteen minutes later with Eggs Benedict. I accepted the plate and thanked her for going to so much trouble.

"No trouble at all," she said.

Her own dish was a cheese omelet and we started in on the food.

"Tell me more about your game plan," Sara requested between mouthfuls.

"Game plan? Who said I have one?"

"You always have one."

I went back to eating.

"Miles?"

"There's a drug called Narvia that, when taken in excess of the prescribed dosage, could cause a person to enter a blackout state and become violent. I need to find out who's taking it." I paused, feeling a pang of guilt in not mentioning I was on the same drug. "Anyway, there's a fine legal line asking people what medications they're on. FBI Agent Diggs is getting a ruling for me."

"Oh—"

"Exactly. Do you see my dilemma? There's no time to waste, yet I can't do anything until I hear back from him."

We finished the rest of our meals in relative silence. Then I stood from the table. "Thanks for brunch, but I have to go to my office, now."

"On a Saturday?" She came to her feet and put her arms around me. "Are you sure you have to go?"

"Sara—"

She planted a sweet kiss on my cheek.

I broke free, though it wasn't easy. "I'll call you later," I said, then left before I changed my mind.

* * *

Halfway to my car the hairs on the back of my neck felt like they were standing on edge. It wasn't all that long ago—at my wife's gravesite in Chicago, to be exact—when I was struck by a similar portent of misfortune, and I ended up being fired not long afterwards.

This felt much worse. I suspected it was due to my feelings for Sara; feelings I hadn't admitted to myself let alone her. There was no reference point, nothing specific I could put my finger on. I couldn't even define it, though I was certain there was something I hadn't yet thought about, something that was destined to effect Sara's future as well as my own.

39

March 25

Denise Gerigk was in her kitchen nibbling on barbecue potato chips and sipping a glass of Chardonnay. She had no plans to step outside, yet she had blow-dried her hair and dressed smartly in a silk blouse and skirt. Wedding ring on her left hand, cocktail ring on the right; tanzanite bracelet with matching necklace. This was just her way. She worked at her appearance and she did it for herself; not to show off, and definitely not to draw attention.

Tom had promised to call at 4:30—fifteen minutes from now—and she was anticipating their conversation. He was back in Toronto, still negotiating with their bank, still suffering from the fallout of Arrow pulling out of Canada, and now worrying what their further loss will be what with Toys Galore just declaring bankruptcy.

The poor man's kidneys were flaring up again, not to mention his back. Was it any wonder, with all the pressure he'd been under? Tom would never admit it but being in his late sixties made it tougher to handle everything. Plus, there was prejudice related to age. Not everyone put relevance in experience. The majority consensus, Denise surmised, was that someone as old as him should have been put out to pasture long ago.

Tom's siblings, a brother seventy-one and a sister sixty-three, lived in Montreal, which left Tom alone in Toronto. This was another reason Denise felt guilty about remaining in Florida while he took on the heavy slogging with their business. But he'd been insistent that she do so, and here she was, grateful but deeply concerned. She placed another chip in her mouth and chased it with a sip of wine.

The portable house phone rang exactly at 4:30; Tom's Germanic precision coming into play. Denise took the receiver in hand and said hello.

"Is it warm?" he asked.

"Warm and beautiful. When're you coming back?"

"I'm not sure. Not for a while yet."

"How come?"

"Too much to do. You know how it is."

"Can't Adrian handle it?" She was referring to Adrian Roche, their VP-Sales, a longtime employee and more than capable of running things on his own.

"I'm afraid not in this situation."

"You mean Arrow?"

"Well—more so the bank."

Denise sighed. "Giving you a hard time?"

"It's this new guy—Bob Cairncross. Robert, he likes to be called. A first-class bastard if ever I saw one."

"What's he saying?"

"*Acht!* it doesn't matter."

"*Acht?*"

"Yeah. That's my Teutonic word for the day."

"So, what did Herr Cairncross tell you?"

"Denise—c'mon. No more business. I'm calling to see how your golf game is doing. Are your friends still upset that you hit the ball straight?"

Denise heard the hitch in her husband's voice. "What are you not telling me, Tom?"

"It's ... nothing."

"*Menteur!* I hate it when you lie to me."

"Denise—"

"No. You listen to me. I'm worried about you. Okay? You can't keep your problems bottled up inside. It's not healthy. What's going on?"

He sighed. "It's worse than I said. With the way the bank is talking, it'll take a miracle to save our business."

Denise felt a twitch in her neck unlike anything she'd experienced before. She moved the phone away from her ear and tried breathing through her mouth. It didn't help. Her neck was locked, the pain intense. Tears came to her eyes.

"Honey?"

She couldn't speak. If she did, Tom would immediately know something was wrong.

"Denise?"

She quick-tapped the off-button on the phone, hoping it'd give the impression of a sudden disconnect; then kept it pressed until she was sure the line had disengaged.

* * *

A few minutes later she recovered sufficiently to text her husband. She lied saying the battery on the phone was near dead and she'd get back in touch sometime the following day.

She spent a fitful night, unable to sleep. In the morning, the pain, while not gone, had eased barely enough for her to function. Denise found she could look left without a problem but not right. To view anything in that direction she had to move her entire body; not an easy or comfortable thing to do.

The more Denise thought about the problem with Tom's business, the more her anxiety level spiked. She paused in the great room by the couch, beside the statue of Jesus on its pedestal, and rubbed it for luck before heading for the bathroom. She stepped inside, filled a glass with water and gulped down a Narvia pill. Then, ignoring the recommended dosage, she swallowed two more.

The newfound energy was unexpected. Denise vacuumed the floor, then dusted some furniture until she began to feel light-headed.

She made it back to the bathroom, where she gripped the edge of the sink and tried to hold herself together. She could no longer feel the pain in her neck; there was too much else going on, especially the palpitations in her chest.

Her strength ebbed. She wanted to stay upright, would give anything to be able to do so. "Why?" she muttered, just before her knees buckled.

* * *

The ceramic tiles on the bathroom floor were cold to the touch; Denise noticed this when she came to before anything else. Then she realized something still wasn't right. Hadn't she read somewhere about the cerebral cortex controlling one's sensory perception? At the moment she had no perception at all.

She got to her feet but couldn't perceive colors. Shapes, too, appeared out of kilter; squares abruptly sliding into circles. There was a buzzing in her ears. Yet, out of the noise came clarity. She left the bathroom, walked awkwardly along the hallway, traversing the great room with care, as if she could lose her balance at any moment.

When she reached the kitchen, Denise paused. *You're procrastinating!* an inner voice insisted.

"Oh my," she said aloud.

An invisible limb gave her a physical shove. Forward, forward, until she stopped in front of the drawers and opened the top one, pulled it out as far as it would go. The butcher knife materialized in her hand.

Denise allowed the sharp edge to run across her forearm. Gently, hardly touching. Then she went at it again; not as gentle this time. She added pressure until this liquid began to flow; dark in color, ominous. *How fascinating!*

40

March 27

I took another sip of coffee; found it was getting cold. This was my second hour searching the web, having filled over five pages in my notebook. Some of what I uncovered was redundant; I'd read about some of the same side effects in the magazines at home. The rest was all new to me, including the number of new medications brought to market each year. When I came upon the extraordinary profits most of the drug manufacturers were earning it made me wonder if someone might be in collusion with a person or persons high up in the FDA. After all, this was a multi-billion-dollar business. It might be the cop in me or the cynic, but I believed that anything was possible. What were the drug manufacturers not telling us? And what were the hidden consequences?

I returned to my computer screen and read on. Six out of ten adults in the United States took some sort of medication. It was closer to nine out of ten for those over sixty-five. In the latter group, four out of ten filled five or more prescriptions. The most commonly used drugs were for high blood pressure and diabetes. Cholesterol and depression weren't far behind.

There was a knock on my office door.

FBI Agent Walter Diggs—dressed smartly in his usual suit and tie, this time in hues of brown—walked in and took a seat. "Pressure's on," he confided. "My boss just called to give me a warning. Unless a serious suspect turns up soon, the Bureau will have to take over."

I leaned forward. "My men are doing everything they can."

"I'm sure they are. I have firsthand knowledge of their work ethic as well as yours. But you can't afford to have anyone else murdered on your watch." He paused and lowered his voice. "Between us, I think Governor Mackie has gotten to the powers that be. The murders are unprecedented, Miles. This case has become a political hot potato."

I didn't say anything for a few seconds. I had the utmost respect for Walter Diggs, but didn't know how far to trust him. Besides, what could I say: *Arrest me. I could be one of the perps?*

I tried another tact. "Walter—I told you my theory about extremely adverse side effects of prescription medication. Is there any word on how far we can take our inquiries?"

"No. Not yet, I'm afraid. But I should have it for you later today."

"Okay, good. Recently, I've narrowed it down to one drug in particular ... Narvia. It's manufactured by Foster Pharmaceuticals, a giant in the drug industry. I'm planning to pay them a visit, but I'll likely need a court order to get them to cooperate."

"How soon?"

"Now."

"Okay. I'll see what I can do," Diggs said. "But step it up, Miles. The clock is ticking."

41

One week prior

Frank Sinclair was on Interstate 24, outside of Chattanooga, Tennessee, when reality smacked him in the face. *What the hell am I doing? Running to my home in St. Louis is not a smart idea, not if I want to be truly safe. Yes, Tracy lives next door; one of the hottest lays of my life. But is she worth the risk? My best bet is to get the hell out of the country.*

He'd vacationed in Bangkok many times and had connections there. Plus, the American dollar went a long way. And no one had to tell him about the women, their desire to please and make any man feel welcome.

Night had fallen and Frank was having trouble staying awake. He still wasn't 100% decided about what he was going to do when he pulled off at the next exit. His eyes automatically went to his rearview mirror. He knew the black van had passed him hours ago, but he still needed to be sure.

Once satisfied the tail was gone, he continued for a quarter mile where he found the Holiday Inn as advertised on a freeway sign. He paid cash and headed for a room on the ground floor.

Less than ten minutes later Frank was in the bar, nursing a Manhattan. The first few sips went down smoothly enough, at a slow, relaxed pace. Then he consumed the rest in three gulps. He swallowed the cherry, while signaling the bartender for a refill.

* * *

Bill Miller, tired as well after driving a full day, picked a Days Inn to spend the night. The long trip had been unexpected and he was not pleased about it. Frank Sinclair's destination had become clear to him by the route he'd chosen, heading toward his hometown of St. Louis. There were other possibilities, of course, but this one made the most sense. Bill handled Frank's financial portfolio; he knew the exact address of his house. He was approximately 150 miles away.

After checking in, he headed to a strip mall and purchased a few necessities: toiletries, a change of underwear, and a heavier jacket; then back to the motel. A familiar twinge in his stomach reminded him that the cancer had no intention of easing up, not even for a minute.

For dinner he had a simple bowl of chicken soup. He awoke early the following morning, looked outside to see snow on the ground. He turned on the news and heard that the temperature had dipped below zero.

Three hours later he was traveling through the outskirts of St. Louis—Clayton and then Ladue. By the time he reached Frontenac he realized he was lost. The van he was driving didn't have a GPS; he had to stop and ask for directions.

Bill finally found his way to Chesterfield, a neighborhood not only populated with mega mansions but newer villa/condos that were becoming the current rage with retirees. A large section of it was still under construction.

He came to a stop on the unpaved road, not quite opposite the address he sought, and waited. From his vantage point, he was able to follow the morning routine: newspapers deposited on a few front porches, mail being delivered. Frank Sinclair's villa remained quiet.

Bill figured that unless Frank drove all night he wouldn't be here yet. To be sure, he put the van in gear and pulled in at the designated parking area. There was no sign of Frank's BMW. But he had no doubt that he was headed here. It didn't matter how long it took. When the man arrived, he'd be ready for him.

Plan A had been to shoot Frank in his car, but with so much traffic and potential witnesses that conception had been replaced with Plan B. The scene played out in his mind: gun at the ready, ring the bell, back Frank inside the house the minute he opened the door. *How I'll enjoy making Frank beg for his life before I pull the trigger. Neighbors won't hear a thing, not with the silencer on the gun. When I leave, I'll say 'goodbye, Frank' and close the door behind me. If anyone's around, I'll smile and wave.*

* * *

Frank slowly came awake; his skull felt three sizes too small for his brain. His throat was parched and he was nauseous. In the shower he figured the cold water would do the trick, and it more or less did. While toweling himself off, however, the room began to spin; he had to brace himself against the wall and wait for the feeling to pass.

Breakfast in the coffee shop was forced down; bacon, eggs and hash browns. Most of the time, one of his favorite meals of the day. But not now. While eating he found it necessary to support his head with his hand.

Back in his room, after brushing his teeth, he made the mistake of lying down on the unmade bed and sleep overtook him. Two hours later his eyes flipped open and he was confused as to where he was. Then he remembered and knew it was decision time.

Part of him wanted to continue on to St. Louis and have a romp with Tracy. But it would have to be quick as he couldn't stay. Bangkok, on the other hand, would not only provide relative safety but a continuous stream of exotic women; drinking and dancing on the beach, plus endless sex.

The image left its mark. He couldn't imagine leaving the country soon enough.

42

March 29

The head office in Manhattan for Foster Pharmaceuticals was exactly what I'd expected to find—ultra-modern, with more glass than steel. Situated downtown in the financial district, it rose fifty stories in an unusual octagonal shape as if it wanted to draw attention to itself.

I'd ridden the elevator to the top floor forty-five minutes ago and here I sat, in the ornate reception area, still waiting, my appointment time of two o'clock long since past.

Most of the magazines on display were drug industry related and I found them boring. I leaned back in the plush upholstered chair and reflected on the latest steps I'd taken to speed up our investigation. Agent Diggs had come through with legal authorization for us to interview residents of Bonita Palms. But there were parameters, restricting us to questions solely about Narvia and limiting the scope of our inquiries.

Meanwhile, it had taken persistence on my part to arrange this interview today. I'd left countless messages for Hugh

Bostwick, the president of Foster, without a reply. But a request for help to Guy Thomas, my old boss with the Chicago police department—now a fast-rising star with the NYPD—secured an appointment. With it, however, had come a succinct warning: "Be on your toes, Miles. I understand Bostwick is quite a character. The man likes to talk down to people, so you might be tempted to say something to piss him off. Do so and I can see your meeting coming to an abrupt end."

I'd read up on the drug industry before coming here. Almost four hundred billion dollars in annual sales in the U.S. alone. I'd also looked into Foster's president. The man was in his early fifties and had built quite a reputation for himself. He was the wunderkind of the drug industry, known for his brash manner with employees and competitors alike. Married for the third time—to a woman half his age—he kept a condo in Manhattan and a home on Long Island's Gold Coast.

"Deputy?"

Automatically, I looked at my watch: 3:05. And here was Hugh Bostwick, himself, out to greet me.

There was no apology for the long wait. The man led the way along a corridor to a corner office that was over forty feet in length. It not only had a cherrywood desk that could seat more than four comfortably but an area opposite that resembled a large living room: black leather couch with three matching chairs facing it, thick pile area rug, wet bar, and a credenza that contained snacks and a broad assortment of wines and liquors.

The president of Foster took a seat on the couch and I chose the chair closest to him.

Bostwick was stocky; barely five-seven, if I had to guess. Brownish hair and blue eyes. He was dressed impeccably in a gray suit, with matching red and gray tie. "Why are you here?" he asked.

"Murder case I'm working on could involve one of your products," I said with a deadpan expression. "I need to know about Narvia and its side effects, other than what's printed on the package."

The president observed me with amusement. "Should I have my lawyer present?"

"Your lawyer?"

"Yes, Deputy. There's something in your tone that sounds accusatory. Every drug we have on the market has been through the most stringent research and testing procedures in the industry. Each and every one of our products is absolutely safe." He paused. "This includes Narvia."

Bullshit, I wanted to say, but I held my tongue, hoping that discretion truly was the better part of valor. "Look—I'm sorry. I didn't mean to insinuate that Foster has done anything wrong. It's just that … well, I have no one else to turn to, to be perfectly frank. I need to know the components of Narvia and how it works in the human body." *And what's being kept hidden from the public.*

The man's smile was insincere. "It would take too long to explain."

"How about the short version?"

Bostwick held his tongue.

I was beginning to think I'd have to use the ace up my sleeve—actually in my pocket—when the president stood and offered me a drink. "Vodka? Scotch?"

"Coffee would be appreciated. Black, please."

Bostwick placed the order with his secretary, requested the

same for himself, then reclaimed his seat. "Tell me about this case of yours."

I kept the story vague but as intriguing as I could manage, concluding with, "Four victims, all women. Murders committed before nightfall by someone each of them knew. We suspect prescription medication played a critical roll in the perpetrator's behavior."

"Narvia?"

"It could be related. Yes."

Both coffees were delivered by a gorgeous twenty-something woman. I assumed she was the one I'd spoken to countless times on the phone, Ms. Berg, who'd refused to put me through to her boss. She was tall with dark hair and a striking face, more suited for a fashion runway than an office.

The minute she departed I asked Bostwick to fill me in on the protocol for bringing a drug to market."

He looked at me like I had two heads. "You wouldn't understand."

"Try me."

"Waste of time."

"I beg your pardon?"

"You heard me."

Easy! the voice in my head cautioned. The warning from my old boss came back, about the man's penchant for talking down to people. "How about the *For Dummies* version?" I requested. "So a simple-minded person like myself can comprehend?"

He gave an exaggerated sigh, then turned to me with disdain in his voice. "Each new substance is screened by organic chemists who try to define its molecular shape and size. Following its initial creation in the test tube, a tiny portion of this substance, amounting to perhaps a few grams, is manufactured. Depending on what area of the body it's intended to work on, elaborate clinical trials are then developed."

"And this would take how long?" I interjected.

He paused, displeased that I'd dared to speak. "It's a tedious process. From time to time—but not often—the Food and Drug Administration here in the United States modernize their approval methods, thereby quickening the process for ratification."

Modernized methods? I wondered if this was the reason so many new medications were approved in the first place. And it made me question the veracity of what we were being led to believe, particularly in advertising.

"If the tests prove positive," Bostwick continued, sounding more like a lecturer than a man attempting a simple explanation, "a larger batch is made and goes into early animal screening."

"Wait a minute," I interrupted again. "What animals are used in these—uh—experiments?"

"They're not experiments. I told you, you wouldn't understand. Acute toxicity studies are developed in rodents. How they behave is crucial, especially if they die. After death they're fully dissected. Organs like brain, liver and heart are examined to try and detect the mode of activity of the drug. When some idea of the safe amount of each compound is determined, the tests begin again. Once fatalities are completely eliminated the decision is made about what animals to use next, be it beagle dogs or sub-human primates such as apes and monkeys."

"And if these poor things should also happen to die?" I couldn't help asking.

Bostwick's face colored noticeably. "You're not listening," his voice rose. "I said *after* fatalities are eliminated."

"Go on…"

"A compound that reaches this stage goes into what is called large batch development. If a drug passes its trials with animals, we are then allowed to proceed with testing in humans. Studies begin with both placebos and the real thing in a select group of volunteers."

The man paused for breath. I was hopeful that the recital was over. When he took a long sip of his coffee and sat back, I realized that it was.

"So, what about my earlier question?"

The man waved me off. "I've told you all you need to know."

"I don't think so," I insisted. If I let this guy have his way, I had no doubt he'd prevaricate to the nth degree, that he'd disseminate, equivocate, do everything in his power to throw me off the scent. "You spoke in generalities. Now let's focus on Narvia. How many prescriptions are sold each year in the U.S.?"

He ignored me, sitting there as if bored, looking every which way except directly at me.

"Sir?"

"The information won't do you a bit of good."

"Let me be the judge of that, if you don't mind. Can you tell me how many are sold?

"How about thousands upon thousands per *month*."

"Per month?" The number floored me.

"Of course. Narvia is a bestseller, at or near the very top of all drugs produced in this country. And we're very proud of its success."

"What are your annual sales?"

"I can't divulge that information."

"You dubbed it a bestseller. Yet everything I read, every

advertisement for Narvia I see on television, comes with a whole slew of warnings that never seem to end. Side effects that appear worse than any disease. Why is this?"

The president ignored the question, stood, and headed toward his desk.

"Sir?"

No response.

I got up and followed. "Mr. Bostwick?"

He took a seat and spoke without looking up. "I have work to do."

In a calm voice I said, "I need the list of pharmacies dispensing Narvia in the Bonita Springs area of Florida."

He shook his head, then spewed arrogance, "Sorry, but I don't have to reveal that information."

I remained composed. "Yes, you do."

Bostwick laughed. "Oh really? And how are you going to make me? With force? Police brutality?" His hand went beneath his desk.

I realized he was probably preparing to hit a secret button that'd have security in the room within seconds.

"I don't need to use force," I shrugged.

He snickered. "Then what?"

"This will do the trick." I removed the subpoena from my jacket pocket and tossed it onto his desk.

"What's this?" His glance went from the document to me, daggers burning into my eyes.

"Read it."

"I don't have time to read it. Why don't you summarize for me?"

"That's a court order instructing you to provide me with the information I need about Narvia."

"So ... I *should* have had my lawyer here, after all!"

"It's not too late. You can call him now. But the subpoena stands, either way."

Bostwick made a move for his phone, then hesitated. I saw the change come over him; like most bullies when it's obvious they no longer have the upper hand. Gone was his flippant attitude. What he said next was spoken with a measure of deference: "What exactly do you want to know?"

I resisted the urge to gloat. "By cooperating with our investigation, you'll be granted immunity from prosecution. I'll contact the FBI and get that in writing for you. Meanwhile, you have time to start damage control. It appears Narvia has an adverse effect only on people with a certain genetic disposition—or possibly in conjunction with another drug. We believe some people who take Narvia, especially those who exceed the recommended dosage, have blackout episodes and become violent. Fortunately, that number is very small."

Bostwick's eyebrow twitched. "And?"

"I need your list of pharmacies who've been prescribing Narvia in the Bonita Springs area of Florida."

"I don't have such a list." he paused. "But I can ask my sales staff to gather it for you." He pointed at the subpoena. "But you'll have to get that amended. The drugstores won't cooperate without legal assurances that they won't be prosecuted for breaking patient confidentiality."

I took out my phone and began texting Walter Diggs, hoping he could have the change made without difficulty.

"Deputy?"

"Sorry. I'm working on your request."

"When do you think you'll have it by?"

My phone chimed. As expected, it was Diggs' reply. I looked at the screen then reported: "Hopefully you'll have it in a day or two. How long will you need once you get it?"

"Not long. I can see there's some urgency. I'll do my best to speed this along." Bostwick paused. "Look—there's no denying I'd be pleased if you're wrong about Narvia. But, however this shakes out, I hope you nail your killer."

"I hope so as well, Mr. Bostwick." I stood, nodded a goodbye. "For both our sakes."

43

March 31

Denise sat on the couch in the great room of her home opposite Brad Pedersen, each holding a glass of iced tea. She self-consciously tugged at the long sleeves of her blouse that hid the self-inflicted cuts along her arms. She didn't know what he'd make of it; she hardly knew what to make of it herself.

"The reason I'm here," Pedersen said evenly, "is to ask if you're taking a prescription medication called Narvia."

She barely understood the question but wasn't about to ask him to repeat it. Denise wasn't herself; hadn't been for the past number of days. She began to wonder if the cause was the very medication the sergeant was talking about.

"Ma'am?" Pedersen queried.

She began to squirm in her seat. "Yes?"

"Did you understand what I just said?"

"Of course," she lied.

"Well, if you're on the pills, have you noticed any adverse side effects? Anything unusual that's happened to you since you began taking them?"

"What's that?"

"Narvia, Mrs. Gerigk?"

"Narvia?" Denise felt off balance. Her mind was entering that other zone, where reason took a holiday, imagining the knife in her hand, cutting herself; the delicious feel of the blade.

Her eyes began to close; she forced them open; noticed her empty glass; an excuse to move; quell her nervous energy. She stood. "Would you like a refill?"

"No thank you, ma'am." He indicated his own glass of iced tea which was still half full.

"Well, if you'll excuse me, I need a little more." She picked up her glass and headed for the kitchen, wobbling slightly along the way.

"Are you okay, Mrs. Gerigk?" Brad called after her.

She stopped, turned back. "I'm … fine," she thought she said, or something to that effect. Then clarity surfaced, and for a moment she knew exactly what she wanted to tell him but, almost immediately, lost her train of thought. Her hand reached out to the nearest drawer. When her fingers touched the butcher knife, she felt a thrill go through her body.

44

April 3

Monday afternoon my four o'clock appointment arrived at my office right on time. Joan Ward and I were familiar with one another. As usual, the bleached blonde was impeccably dressed; pink blouse, and suit an off-white color that was form-shaped.

I invited her to have a seat and asked how I could be of help.

She appeared nervous and took a moment before replying: "I've—uh—come here on my own to give you a warning. The natives are restless. There's talk of the men forming a vigilante committee to do a search and seizure of any suspicious looking characters. I've heard that gun sales have gone through the roof. People are almost at a state of 'Shoot first—ask questions later.' The community has dubbed you guys 'The Keystone Cops'."

I could see how difficult this was for her, but I was caught between a rock and a hard place. If I didn't make a public announcement of my Narvia theory, another murder might occur. But if I did broadcast it, the serial killer would likely stop taking it—lose the urge to do harm—then essentially disappear. This would leave Bonita Palms with a series of unsolved murders that would haunt the community for years to come. Even if the killing spree stopped, the residents of the Palms would never feel truly safe and would always have to be on guard. And then there was Murphy's Law—exactly when they did begin to relax, believing the killer's lust had been satisfied, he would then strike again.

"Mrs. Ward—"

"Joan," she corrected.

"Joan, I can understand the frustration. But this type of investigation, where there's no evident motive, is the most difficult to solve. My men have been working nonstop, approaching each murder from various angles, all without the results we were hoping for. But ... new information has come to light that I'm not at liberty to discuss right now. We have a very promising development and I'm confident this will lead to an arrest."

Mrs. Ward looked up, hesitated, then spilled it out: "Not good enough, I'm afraid. It's been months since the first murder and there's been no progress. People are asking why the investigation is taking so damn long." She blushed. "Sorry. Those aren't my words. My neighbors are saying you're not working hard enough, that you should be doing more to protect us." She paused.

When she spoke again there was a hitch in her voice. "Four of my friends have been murdered. I ... don't sleep at night. I can't eat. I don't feel safe anymore." Another pause. "I've been going out less and less. I've never been claustrophobic before, but the walls of my house keep closing in on me. I feel like I—"

Tears came to her eyes, which caught me off guard. I jumped up and came around the desk, placed my hand on her shoulder, gently squeezed.

"I'm sorry," she apologized, wiping her eyes with a tissue.

"Nothing to be sorry about," I said, remaining by her side.

"I feel terrible for talking to you this way. I know you're doing what you can. But my friends and I are living on the edge. I don't know how much longer we can go on like this."

I weighed her comment for a moment, decided to take her into my confidence. "I believe the killer lives in Bonita Palms and definitely has the trust of the community. But the worst part is, he might not even be aware of what he's doing."

"What do you mean?"

"He could be having a drug-induced breakdown."

"Then how will you catch him?"

"I would like to ask you to be vigilant. Nothing should be taken for granted. A person might do something strange. They could be rude, abrupt, or act in a way that goes against their nature. The behavior pattern I'm suggesting could be subtle and easily dismissed, especially if it's exhibited by someone you know, someone close to you, someone you trust. Look—I'd like to give you my cell number. You'll be able to reach me 24/7."

Mrs. Ward opened her purse and removed her iPhone. I noticed her hands were shaking.

I read my number to her. "I don't want you to put yourself in harm's way looking for a suspect. But should something come to you, don't hesitate to call me. Your name will be protected. Anything revealed to me will be handled with the strictest of confidence."

"All right," she said, but she looked distracted.

"Is there something else I can help you with?"

"No. Not at the moment." She got up but seemed reluctant to leave.

"Mrs. Ward?"

"Oh? I'm sorry. I was thinking about what you said. There *was* something that momentarily occurred to me, but now it's gone. I'm certain it'll come back. Eventually…"

"Let me know if you remember it. Reach out to me at any time, no matter how insignificant it may seem."

45

One week prior

Bill Miller ran out of patience. He'd spent another restless night, this time at a Hampton Inn; his medication losing its effectiveness. The temperature in St. Louis was colder than yesterday, with snow starting to fall again. He drove to Frank's house and pulled up in front. There was no sign of activity inside.

He looked at his watch. Frank should have been here by now. Bill wondered if he'd guessed wrong, if Frank could've been headed somewhere else. But this was the only destination that made sense. Unless ... something happened to him?

Bill returned to the van and checked the monitoring device; nothing registered. He drove down the block and parked. There were a few other cars, none of which belonged to Frank. The snow was picking up. He had no doubt that driving conditions would soon worsen. Frank might be unable to get here. And Bill realized that if his pain grew any worse, he'd have to check himself into the nearest hospital.

*　*　*

A full hour had passed. The knot in Bill's stomach became unbearable. He pulled his Celenome medication out of his pocket. His prescribed limit was two pills per day. This would be his fourth. He popped it into his mouth and dry swallowed.

The snow was now obstructing the van's windshield, making it impossible to see. Bill started the motor and put on the wipers. But he couldn't let the van idle for long. Twice before it had overheated. He waited a few minutes. Sure enough, the temperature gauge began to move toward the danger zone. Bill shut off the motor, opened the door and stepped out, grateful for the jacket he'd purchased yesterday. He began to brush the snow off the windshield with his hands until they grew so cold he could hardly feel them. He cupped his fingers and blew on them, which didn't do much good. The snow was relentless. Trying to wipe it all away was a losing cause.

Bill went to get back in the van when he slipped and fell. His right leg hit the icy ground at an awkward angle and a ferocious pain shot up his spine. He called for help but realized he was too far away for anyone to hear him. *Get your phone out,* he told himself, but his hands wouldn't obey. Then the irony hit him, that Frank Sinclair would survive while he would not.

46

April 3
Early evening

In bed with Sara after making love, feeling her warmth against my chest, gave me a feeling of such contentment, I longed for it to last forever.

"What's going on?" she asked.

"Nothing."

"So why the Cheshire cat grin?"

I wanted to tell her how happy she made me feel, that I more than cared about her.

"Miles?"

"Shh—" I snuggled closer.

I wasn't supposed to be here. I'd called her right after Joan Ward had left my office and voiced my concern about the Bonita Palms residents running out of patience. Sarah understood my frustration, invited me over for dinner, and wouldn't take no for an answer.

I arrived in an uptight state of mind. Sara answered the door wearing nothing but bikini panties and a spaghetti-strapped white camisole with the word "appetizer" printed in black across the front.

I stood there, speechless. At first. Then I began to laugh, loud and hard, longer than I'd laughed in months ... until tears came to my eyes.

"Do you like?" Sara batted her eyelashes.

I more than liked.

She beckoned with an index finger and I followed, from the foyer of the house to her bedroom, where the lights were off and a lone candle burned.

Sara became playful, made a show of removing the flimsy undergarments she had on. I caught sight of the butterfly-shaped birthmark above her naval. She pushed me onto the bed and began to undress me, slapping my hands away when I tried to help.

I'd recently stopped taking my Narvia medication. On the one hand, my anxiety was slowly creeping back. But on a positive note, I'd experienced no further blackout episodes. As a result, I felt confident there wouldn't be a repeat of what happened the last time she'd joined me in bed.

I started to expound upon this, but Sara hushed me, saying, "I'm not worried."

We made love in a manic frenzy. Then, after catching our breath, we went at it again, slower this time, teasing each other and making it last.

* * *

I slept for a while, woke to the sound of Sara working in the kitchen. By the time I joined her she had the room lights dimmed and the dining room table set.

"Sit, sleepyhead," she said.

I sat.

There was a bowl in front of me.

"Butternut squash soup," Sara announced. "I hope you like it. I prepared everything in a rush. Not sure how good it's going to taste."

I looked at the bowl, then at Sara. I was in love with this woman but couldn't figure out how to tell her. I waited until she was seated before spooning my first mouthful.

"Yum. Terrific." I rubbed my stomach.

"You're just saying that to make me feel good."

"No, I'm not."

"If I ever catch you lying to me, mister, I'll be forced to reprimand you," she winked.

"Is that a good thing or bad?"

"You don't want to find out."

The entree was linguini in a marinara sauce, and it was delicious as well. I never tired of watching Sara eat, full fist still gripping her fork. In lieu of serving the apple pie I noticed sitting on the counter, Sara stood, leaned toward me, and began to unbutton my shirt.

"Hey, what're you doing, lady?"

"Getting you ready for dessert."

My cell rang. It was in my coat, hanging by the door. I ignored it, not wanting to spoil the moment.

It rang again.

Sara went over, removed it from the pocket and handed it to me.

I glanced at the name—Diggs. I showed it to Sara, said, "Thanks. I'd better take this."

She nodded. "Of course."

"Miles—" The FBI agent's voice was severe enough for me to know it was bad news. "I'm sorry, but the plug is being pulled. I've been instructed to advise you that my team is preparing to take over."

"How long do I have?"

"Until Friday night."

"Huh?" I slapped the table with an open palm.

"Until—"

"I heard you! Goddamnit, Walter, I thought you'd give me a bit of a warning."

"I just gave it to you."

"That's not a warning. I need a week or two, not three days."

"I'm sorry. That's the best I could bargain for. The chief wanted me to take command today."

Don't shoot the messenger, I reminded myself. "Okay, Walter." I hit the OFF button, stood, and turned to Sara. "I've got to go."

"Bad news?"

"The worst. I've been put on the clock."

"Anything I can do?"

"I wish there was." I threw up my hands. "What I need right now is a miracle."

47

April 4

Joan Ward tossed and turned for most of the night, finally getting up at 6 a.m., trying to make as little noise as possible so as to not wake her husband, Seth. She felt an oncoming headache and knew the reason why, continuously racking her brain for something that remained elusive.

She took a quick shower, got dressed in a rose-colored cotton sweater and three-quarter length capris. Barefoot, she strolled into the kitchen where she made herself a decaf coffee, along with two pieces of whole wheat toast with strawberry jam.

The blinds were seldom drawn so she had a perfectly clear view of her lanai, brilliantly lit now by the sun, already blessing this part of Florida with what many considered an elixir of good cheer.

Bah, humbug, Joan thought. *This getting old is for the birds.* She never considered herself to be a flake. She could remember things that happened years ago as if they occurred yesterday, but something from last month, last week, even last hour? Forget about it.

When she met with Deputy Miles a recollection came to her, something she believed to be important, an incident triggered by the man's mention of not overlooking the most innocuous incident. Yet now, a day later, she still couldn't shake it loose.

Joan completed her breakfast and placed the dishes in the sink. Then she took pen and pad in hand and returned to the kitchen table. She wasn't going to allow depleting memory cells to defeat her. It was one thing to not have the stamina she once had, to not have anywhere near the energy, vitality, or even the patience of the woman she was a few short years ago. But this—whatever it was—knowing it could be important, would not be allowed to remain elusive much longer.

She began as if writing a diary, going back three months, noting the date and copying down everything she could remember that occurred. Some things were easy, like when she played golf or bridge. Others not as much, like where she and Seth went to dinner the Saturday before last.

Her page quickly filled up. When there was no room left, she stood from the table, balled the sheet of paper in her fist and threw it toward the wastebasket, but missed. She glared at it, let it remain on the floor, a reminder of her ineptitude. No matter what, she would not give up. Even though it might all be for naught. Her frustration could rage on; she didn't care. One way or another, she would force her mind to spit out what she was looking for. And then she would determine if it was meaningful or not.

48

The same day

I entered my office and took a seat behind my desk. My head reeled with the realization that there were three days left for me to solve the murder case, or at the very least, come up with a likely suspect. Having the FBI take over would be a mistake. Based on what Diggs had told me, the Feds had their own methodology for running an investigation. One based on facts, not *theories*. They'd likely start from scratch and re-interview all the workers, using their more thorough techniques. I was afraid they'd end up taking *more* time rather than *saving* time.

I'd forwarded Hugh Bostwick the amended subpoena he requested. The next day, I received a short, preliminary list of people in Bonita Springs who had filled Narvia prescriptions in recent weeks, with a promise of more to come. Five names in all. There was no explanation as to why the list was incomplete. I assumed Foster's president wanted to get something to me quickly to shut me up. But the clock was ticking.

Pedersen and Wellington stepped into my office, right on

time for our 10 a.m. meeting. I noticed Brad could barely contain himself and asked what was going on.

He reviewed the results of the interviews he'd conducted and said all were cooperative and readily gave up the information that was asked of them. Of course, he couldn't push too hard because of the narrow guidelines Walter Diggs was able to get the court to approve.

"But that's not what's got you worked up," I noted.

"No, it's not," he concurred. "Denise Gerigk and I have met on various occasions, chiefly at the charity events we both volunteer for. But when I interviewed her the other day, she acted like she hardly knew me. She was distant and cold, sort of spacey."

"Were you able to find out if she's using Narvia?"

"She wouldn't say right away. But I noticed there were cuts on her arms. Some were healing—others looked fresh. We were seated across from each other. She kept fidgeting with her blouse, trying to pull the sleeves lower. In my estimation, the wounds were self-inflicted.

"Anyway, at one point she stood up and ostensibly went to the kitchen to get herself a refill of iced tea. Next thing I see she's pulling a knife out of a drawer and—to best describe it—I'd say she was *fondling* it. Without moving her head, her eyes shot a look my way. But I couldn't say for sure what she was thinking. Could it have been a desire to use the knife on herself? Or was she considering using it on me?"

I felt this little thrum in my brain. "And she is on Narvia?"

"Yes, she is. But she said she experienced no side effects that she could recall."

I liked and respected Denise Gerigk. Was it a coincidence that a knife was used on our latest victim and Mrs. Gerigk seemed obsessed with knives? How should I interpret her odd behavior? Weren't the FBI profilers convinced our perp was male?

Go slow, an inner voice cautioned. *Don't be blinded by your desperate need for a resolution.*

Still … side effects from drugs knew no gender bias. At the very least, didn't this warrant further inquiry on my part?

* * *

After dismissing the others, I sat alone in my office, door closed. They had brought me up to speed before leaving. The two service contractors—Turk Lagerfeld of Comcast and Harold Brown of Florida Power and Light—had been looked at from every conceivable angle and were finally cleared. Meanwhile, Frank Sinclair hadn't been seen in weeks. I always thought he made a good suspect. If we still couldn't reach him by the end of the day, I'd have to consider issuing an APB. His alibi was solid for his wife's murder but not for any of the others. Besides, if he wasn't Cathy's actual killer, who's to say he didn't hire a professional killer to eliminate her and perhaps one or two more to make it look like the work of a serial killer?

So where does that leave us?

Unfortunately, with four suspects: #1—unknown, #2—Frank Sinclair, #3—Mrs. Gerigk, #4—myself. This meant I had to go nonstop over the three days left to me, pressing the hunt into an entire new gear.

* * *

I called the office and cell numbers I had for Hugh Bostwick; both went to voicemail, so I left messages. I needed the full list he promised, not a meager sampling of five names. I turned on my computer and tried searching out whatever background information I could find on Mrs. Gerigk. Google helped but it wasn't enough. Finally, I called an old acquaintance of mine—Jean Brunel, a lieutenant with *Sûreté du Québec*—and explained what I needed.

"Give me an hour," the genial Brunel said.

"One hour?" I asked in surprise.

"*Bien sur.* Unless you want me to take longer?"

"No, no. An hour would be wonderful. I didn't think you could accomplish much on such short notice."

"Have you forgotten whom you're dealing with, *mon ami?*"

I laughed. Jean and I had worked a case many years ago when I was with Chicago PD. A brutal drug dealer who had slipped our grasp and made his way into Canada was brought to justice within 24 hours by my fast-acting cohort.

"I didn't forget," I told him. "I'd really appreciate your magic touch one more time."

"You'll get it. I promise."

49

One week prior.

Frank Sinclair headed south on I-75 and took the University Parkway exit for Sarasota. Fifteen minutes later he arrived at the non-gated community of Saddlebrook. Frank had maintained a pied-à-terre here for the past five years. A small condo to escape to without prying eyes, where he could carry on his assignations without his wife or anyone else being the wiser. It was 1,200 square feet on the lower level of a triplex; all the amenities without the hassle or the upkeep of a private home.

He drove into the garage and parked, then made his way into the condo, where he dumped his car keys onto the kitchen counter. Without pausing he stepped up to the cupboard, removed the bottles of red and white CinZano, along with the bottle of Canadian Club. The first Manhattan of the day always tasted best. But before he could pour the drink, Frank realized time was of the essence. *Move. Move before it's too late.*

He left the bottles where they were and raced into the bedroom, dumping the contents of his travel bag onto the bed.

Within minutes he had everything repacked into a suitcase: a change of clothes, fresh underwear, shirts and socks, the usual toiletries.

Frank didn't know if a warrant had been issued for his arrest and, if it had been, how far-reaching that warrant might be. It could cover the area between Naples and Fort Myers which included Bonita Springs, or it could extend even farther, across all of Florida, possibly all of the United States.

He figured going to the airport in Sarasota without using a disguise would be sheer stupidity. His name and a photo could be on a "no-fly" list. Anything was possible.

Frank unlocked the strongbox he kept in his bedroom closet and removed $12,000 in cash. That and the $20,000 he'd taken from his hidden stash at his home in Bonita Palms should keep him going for a while. He also collected the fake passport he'd used once before, when he believed Cathy was rightfully suspicious about a trip he had planned to the Hedonism Resort in Jamaica with his latest sexual conquest. He'd purchased the passport under the name of James Deverol through a drinking buddy, whose contacts included an underworld figure whom Frank was better off knowing nothing about.

He stepped into the bathroom and removed a wig and moustache from the bottom drawer of the cabinet. This purchase was made from a men's salon noted for their quality, and not shy in charging an exorbitant price for their discretion. Black, longer, and styled vastly different from his own artificially-enhanced brown hair, it took Frank a few minutes to be sure the glue adhered properly to his skin and that the look closely resembled his passport photo.

He walked a few blocks to the bus stop, and thirty minutes

later disembarked a short stroll from the main entrance of the Sarasota/Bradenton International Airport. The female clerk at JetBlue, the official operator in this part of the country for Qatar Airways—an average-looking woman around his own age—raised a wary eyebrow as he counted out the $6,300 in cash for his Business Class ticket.

Frank was normally not one to remain on edge, but he felt uncomfortable in his disguise. Still, he made direct eye contact with the agents when he went through security and also with the flight attendants when he boarded the aircraft. *Play it cool*, he reminded himself throughout his layover in Boston and his stopover in Qatar. After boarding the last leg of his trip to Bangkok, he finally gave himself a self-congratulatory pat on the back. He'd not only escaped Florida but was certain that the payoff—young, eager-to-please girlies—were awaiting him at the end of his long, insufferable journey.

50

April 5

The Air Canada flight from Fort Myers got me into Montreal before noon. The Ford Taurus I rented at Hertz had a GPS, but it spoke French … until I realized there was a way to switch it to English.

The city truly was the Paris of North America, but I didn't have time to enjoy it. The FBI were set to take over the murder case on Friday night, which left me very little breathing room.

Jean Brunel had gotten back to me and explained the need to come to Canada. I tried to argue against. The last thing I wanted was be away from my office.

"You won't accomplish anything by phone," he'd said. "The person you'll be seeing doesn't speak English. On the phone it'll be impossible to understand her or for her to understand you. I've arranged for an interpreter. Drop everything and fly up here. And let me know how it turns out."

I was early so I cruised along Rue St. Germain, south of Sherbrooke, until I came to the house where Denise Gerigk, née

Bernier, was born. A working-class neighborhood, with duplexes and triplexes for the most part, jammed together, uniform in style—mostly dull brown brick—without much in the way of green space ... or any space to speak of at all between buildings.

There was still a little snow on the ground, temperature in the low forties. I'd forgotten about Canadian winters and how they often lingered well into spring.

I checked my watch; time to move on. I entered the address I was given into the GPS and ten minutes later pulled up at L'école Notre Dame de L'Assomption, an old school standing near the corner of Hochelaga and St. Germain.

Sister Therese St. Claire had to be in her early eighties. She was tall, dressed in a nun's black habit adorned with a silver cross. She appeared frail until she shook my hand with such surprising strength I was taken aback. Beside her was another nun, sixtyish, of average height, with expressive, deep blue eyes. The translator.

They led the way to an office—no bigger than eight-by-ten—where Sister St. Claire cleared a handful of French Bibles off the lone chair facing her desk so that I might have a seat. There were a few files, a black rotary-dial telephone, and a Tiffany lamp. The second nun remained standing and introduced herself in near-perfect English: "I am Sister Diane Labelle. It is a pleasure to meet you, *monsieur*."

St. Claire spoke in French and I waited for Sister Labelle's translation: "We understand this is about a past student of ours—Denise Bernier. Here—" I was handed a school yearbook. "Third girl on the left."

I took the book in hand. The photograph vaguely resembled the Denise Gerigk of today. Blonde hair worn longer, face more narrow. She was a member of a high school class, most likely grade nine or ten. About thirty students, all girls, each wearing a white blouse and Blackwatch skirt, with three-quarter length navy socks.

For the next few minutes Sister St. Claire's French was followed by Sister Labelle's translation into English:

"I taught her throughout high school. One of the sweetest pupils you can imagine. Until her father died, that is. Then she changed. Started running with a wild crowd. We tried to help her, me and the other Sisters. She wouldn't listen. Time and again we met with her mother, but the poor woman was in a terrible state herself. Her husband's death had come so suddenly, without warning.

"Her brother and both sisters were also affected, as you can imagine, but were able to cope a lot better. You see, there was quite a difference in age between them and Denise. Being older, they were more … mature. Especially the boy." St. Claire's paused and I noticed her eyes glossing over. She spoke again and I waited for the translation: "Pierre, her brother, had such a way about him. Her sisters—Monique and Sylvie—not so much."

There was a musty smell in the small office making me uncomfortable, though I couldn't afford to rush. "You mentioned a change in Denise. Can you be more specific?"

St. Claire said, *"Les drogues."*

I didn't need a translation. "Drugs?"

"Yes. Not only taking them, but she started to … traffic on them?"

"She was selling drugs to whom?"

St. Claire shrugged when she heard my question transposed into French. "The girls in her class mostly. Maybe to others."

"Others? You mean to total strangers?"

Sister St. Claire clamped up. Something unspoken passed between her and Sister Labelle and neither would look directly at me. I figured there was a secret to be learned, but how to get it out of them?

The silence became uncomfortable. An invisible clock started to tick in my head when Therese St. Claire began a long discourse about Denise's brother:

"Pierre had such manners. There were few like him. Smart. And what athleticism. The boy could skate ... and play hockey. Captain of the school team. The highest scorer for two years in a row. There was even talk of Les Canadiens showing an interest. And then his father died; Pierre was never the same. No one in their family was the same."

I could see the nun held a soft spot for the boy. But she was putting me on. She knew it and I knew it. This was a stalling tactic, yet I could do nothing about it.

Then she stood, spoke, and the translator said: "Thank you for coming here today. That's all she can tell you."

I remained seated. St. Claire eyed me strangely.

"I need more information," I said calmly. "Four women have been murdered. More may die if I don't find a way to stop this madness. I need to hear whatever else you have to say, even if it's confidential. You have my word it will remain between us."

Sister St. Clair took her seat again, folded her hands and waited.

"Just a few more questions," I said. "Was Denise Bernier ever arrested?"

"Not that I know of," was St. Claire's reply.

"What sort of trouble did she get into?"

"It was all a mistake."

"What was?"

"It was long ago. Teenage girls can be so ... vulnerable. With the sudden death in the family, Denise had no one to turn to. I tried to ... take her on my wing, if that is the correct expression. I invited her to help around the school, to do volunteer work. And she did ... but it didn't last.

"Seven months after her father's passing, she disappeared. Her mother became very upset. The police were called, of course. We all thought something had happened to her. None of us believed she would run off on her own.

"No word for two weeks, then news came about a body found in the east-end, down by the port. A man in his early twenties ... a Monsieur Taillebois."

"And Taillebois was into drug trafficking?"

"*Les drogues* ... and selling young girls."

"He was into prostitution?" I wanted clarification.

"*Oui.*"

"How did he die?"

"*Coupé plusieurs fois avec un poignard.*" She paused. "*C'était vraiment un crime passionnel.*"

Now even the translator was speaking French, and I had to wait.

"I'm sorry," she apologized. "Taillebois was stabbed several times with a knife. The police believed it was a crime of passion."

"And?"

St. Claire became reticent again.

"Sister?"

She shrugged. "There wasn't enough evidence to make an arrest."

I looked at the translator, then at her. "What are you not telling me?"

The nuns remained quiet.

I didn't move, allowing the silence to sit between us.

Then Sister Labelle said: "At some point, *before* the murder, Denise had confessed something to St. Claire."

"Oh? What was that?"

"It is difficult for Sister St. Claire to tell you. What Denise said to her is no different from saying it to a priest in the confessional booth."

"I understand that. But the information could save someone's life, Sister."

St. Claire swallowed hard and finally revealed the secret she'd been holding back: "Denise Bernier confessed that she and Taillebois were lovers."

51

The same day

Randal Park under a dark sky, rain pouring down, heat and humidity on hiatus. No neighbors or friends in sight. No one else willing to bear the elements. Solitude as a salve: no one to criticize, nothing to act as a distraction.

The voices are as strident and determined as ever, the difference being that you are now resolved to what they have to say. Relief is guaranteed, just around the corner. Being anxious won't help; it never does.

You stand at the edge of the pond, rain drenching your head and face but not noticing. You're here to put a stop to it, that infinitesimal spot of conscience that hasn't completely dimmed. Ending it is the best way. A plunge into the water, then eternal release.

But the pills you dry swallowed in the car finally begin to take effect and it's not long before you realize that there's more work to do.

Your preference is passivity over action … until it isn't. Until whatever that certain something is inside takes over and there's little choice left, a thrill to experience over and over again.

The physicality of the movement is feared yet cherished. The itch is intense and irresistible. Eyes remain open until a downward pressure closes them. Visualizing before experiencing, waiting and anticipating.

Whew—that was close, you tell yourself. *Thank God for Narvia.* You head back to your car.

There's one more who needs to die!

52

April 7 and 8

I got out of bed Thursday morning after barely sleeping again. The minute I'd left my meeting yesterday afternoon with Sister St. Claire I called Jean Brunel, recapped my interview, and asked for more details about the murder that took place years ago. Jean said he'd see what he could find and get back to me, which he did as soon as I arrived at the Hertz counter at Pierre Elliott Trudeau International Airport.

"What can you tell me?" I asked.

"There's not much, I'm afraid. A cold case rarely gets any warmer. The victim, Paul Taillebois, twenty-one, was the alleged head of a prostitution ring, though never proven. His murder remains unsolved."

"Was a connection between him and Denise Bernier ever substantiated?"

"Just rumors that they were lovers. Apparently, Denise discovered he was two-timing her. Still, no hard evidence that she did the deed. The fingerprints were wiped clean from the knife.

Denise's DNA was found on his body but so was that of another unidentified woman's. Either one could have been the killer. And since the victim was a drug dealer, there was also the possibility it was a robbery gone bad."

I thanked Jean for his help and promised to have lunch or dinner with him next time I was in Montreal. Then I contacted Brad Pedersen and explained what I needed done.

I didn't hear back from Brad until I landed in Fort Myers. Denise Gerigk was tied up with a doctor's appointment she couldn't cancel but had agreed to see me Friday morning. I told myself I'd best start preparing. Sometimes the stars aligned, and I believed they were doing so now. But this was going to take all the guile I possessed. One way or another, the burden rested with me to entrap a killer.

***

When I arrived home last night from the Fort Myers airport, I received an email from Hugh Bostwick finally listing the balance of residents in Bonita Springs who'd filled recent prescriptions for Narvia. A total of forty names.

Before I could decide how to handle investigating them, I took a call from Sara, welcoming me back.

"I was only gone for one day," I reminded her. "You make it sound like I was away for a week."

"Well, I missed you."

"Thanks. I missed you as well."

"It seems we're always saying that to each other. Wouldn't it be nice if we had a more permanent arrangement?"

"Sara—"

"You can give a girl a complex, Miles."

I could see her point, but the jury was still out on my involvement in one or more of the murders. Until the killer or killers were found I couldn't commit to a future with her. "This case is really weighing me down," was all I could say.

There was a pause. "I understand."

"You do? I appreciate that, Sara." I tried to stifle a yawn.

"Not getting much sleep," she noted.

I told her what was happening.

"Forty names?"

"That's right. Plus the five on the original list. Meanwhile, Walter Diggs was called away to FBI Headquarters in Tampa to discuss the takeover of our case, and Wellington and Pedersen are at an all-day police conference in Miami. This leaves me alone until Friday, which is our deadline. I don't see how we'll be able to cover everyone. It's damn near imposs—"

"Did you say Friday?" Sara interrupted. "That's my day off. I can help … if you want me to."

I hesitated. "I'm not sure…"

"Not sure about what? Just tell me what time you want me there."

* * *

Thursday passed like the calm before the storm. I chose names on the list I was familiar with, and spent time interviewing each one in their homes. I listened to complaints about anxiety, but no one said anything suspicious or acted in a way that would cause me to view them as a suspect.

At home that night I reheated a chicken dish I'd been saving and gobbled it down. Today's interviews had led me in the direction of liking Denise as the primary suspect; or if there were more, at least one of them.

I was in bed by eleven but remained awake, wondering what I'd do if tomorrow's interviews didn't lead to a suspect.

When I awoke on Friday a feeling of trepidation stayed with me throughout the routine of shower and shave, then breakfast. I figured with Sara we'd have a chance of completing all interviews in the one day. But I was certain I'd missed something, a puzzle-like piece floating in the ethernet of my mind.

The minute I opened the door to my car my cell rang. Unknown name, unknown number. I was about to answer when the phone slipped out of my hand and fell onto the driver's seat. By the time I picked it up it had stopped ringing. No message left. I arrived at my office and a second call came in. This time I was distracted by Sara just coming through the door, so I missed that one as well.

Once she was seated, along with Pedersen and Wellington, I handed out the lists I'd created for each member of the team including myself, having split the names four ways. After the eight I covered yesterday, plus the original five, we were left with eight each.

"I'm interviewing Mrs. Gerigk first," I announced. "She's my prime. If something comes of it, I'll reach out to all of you. Be sure to have your cell phones on. In the meantime, remember—you have to be careful not to overstep your legal authority. You can ask how long they've been taking Narvia and if they've experienced any unusual side effects. You can also ask about their whereabouts on the days and times each murder took place. If you come across anything highly unusual, or anyone looking suspicious, take whatever necessary precautions, then call me. Any questions?"

There were none and we all filed out of my office.

*　*　*

Throughout the drive I concentrated on how I could work a confession out of Mrs. Gerigk. Most of us in law enforcement have our own patented methods. Some acted the roll of accuser, then priest. I usually played it straight and aboveboard, aiming to convince the doer of the old adage: *The truth shall set you free.*

A flash of lightening lit up the sky followed by a loud clap of thunder. Then rain, accompanied by a strong wind. I could feel the car shake as I drove up to the security gate at Bonita Palms.

A new rent-a-cop I hadn't seen before waved me through. I reached the Gerigk home in Augusta a few minutes later and parked behind a car that looked familiar, yet I couldn't place it.

The rain eased up. I was about to get out of my vehicle when my phone rang. I examined the screen: unknown name, unknown number. I ignored it. This wasn't the time to be distracted. Almost at the entrance to the Gerigk residence it went off again. This time it was my office, so I accepted the call.

"Sir—" the desk sergeant said, "there's a woman looking for you: Joan Ward. She's apparently been trying to reach you all morning and says that it's urgent."

"Did she tell you what it's about?"

"Something you mentioned at a recent meeting you had with her. Would you like her number?"

"Yes, please."

I vacillated between returning the call now or later; decided on now and punched in the digits.

"Hello?"

"Mrs. Ward?"

"Yes. This is Joan."

"Miles Delany. I understand you've been trying to reach me?"

"Yes, I have. I've called you a few times this morning. I've been racking my brain trying to remember an incident that happened to me recently. I felt it was my duty to tell you about it." She hesitated.

"Go on, Mrs. Ward," I prompted her.

"You told me I should be on the lookout for anyone who acts in a way that goes against their nature."

"That's true."

"You also said any information I pass along would be held in the strictest of confidence."

"Also true."

"Well, I have a concern about one of my neighbors."

I took a deep breath. "Go on."

"I hope you won't think I'm being foolish."

"Ma'am," I said, anxious to move her along, "believe me, I'm grateful for the call. I don't mean to be rude, but can you get to the point?"

"Some time ago—not sure exactly when—I was home alone and had an unexpected visitor. I remember it being close to the dinner hour…"

A chill went up my spine. *Dinner hour? The same time each of the murders took place.*

"I explained that my husband was out, but she was welcome to stay and visit."

She? I was right … Denise.

"The moment she stepped inside, however, she began acting strange. Barely a peep out of her except to say she'd like a glass of water, with ice. Off I went to the kitchen to prepare some hors d'oeuvres. Can't simply offer a glass of water to a guest. But I could swear she was bothered about something. Really bothered. And when I came back with the tray, she was gone. Not only that, but the front door was left wide open. There was no 'goodbye', no 'sorry something came up and I have to go'. She disappeared … just like that."

I heard Mrs. Ward snap her fingers.

"Do you think I'm being silly for calling you?" she asked warily.

"No. Not at all," I said, my pulse starting to gallop. My suspicion of Mrs. Gerigk as the prime suspect was about to be confirmed. "Can you tell me the name of your visitor?"

"Do you promise to keep me out of it?"

"You have my assurance, Joan. Who was it?"

"Debbie Stafford. I don't know if you know her. She lives—"

Debbie Stafford? Disbelief washed over me. I was stunned. This was not the name I expected to hear.

"Sheriff—do you know where she lives?"

"Yes, I do." I pictured Mrs. Stafford in my mind, remembering the times I'd been summoned to her home; the woman fading in and out of reality, seeing ghosts. "Thanks very much for the information, Joan. It will be kept in strict confidence." I disconnected before I could be delayed any further.

I removed the master list I kept in my pocket and gave it a hard look. Within seconds I was swearing to myself. The Stafford residence was under Sara's name and it was her first interview.

I dialed her cell as fast as I could; it went to voicemail. I got a hold of Brad. "Get to the Stafford house!" I instructed, fighting my panic. "Drop everything and move. Call Wellington on your way. Get him over there too. Now!"

* * *

I was first to arrive. Sara's beige SUV was the only vehicle in sight. I very much wanted to believe Debbie Stafford wouldn't be capable of murder, that I was jumping to conclusions. But all I could do now was pray I'd find Sara safe and sound.

I parked behind her SUV and hurried out. It was eerily quiet. The rain had stopped and the wind had abated, yet the sky was dark.

I approached the door; found it unlocked. I thrust it open. The lights were off, I couldn't make out much of anything. "Sara?" I called.

I remembered the plan of the house from the many times I'd been there. The abundance of crosses and crucifixes on the walls. The rooms standing kitty-corner to the entranceway.

I fanned a bank of light switches with my hand, then moved forward. "Mr. and Mrs. Stafford," I called out. "I need you both to show yourselves."

No response.

I searched the great room; made my way in and out of each bedroom and bathroom, then the rooms Debbie and Larry used as individual offices. There was no sign of anyone, and I knew time was running out on Sara.

In the hallway I felt a slight breeze and traced its source. The sliding doors leading to the lanai had been left open. It took a few quick strides to get there. The sky wasn't much brighter but I could make out the pool, the sauna and built-in barbecue. Everything seemed in order.

I hurried back into the house. If Sara's SUV was out front, where was she? And where were Mr. and Mrs. Stafford? I forced down a growing sense of dread and retraced my steps. The last place I hadn't looked was the garage.

I reached it in seconds. There were two spaces, both empty. I tried to picture the vehicle Mrs. Stafford drove, a white Jag ... and immediately knew why the car parked outside the Gerigk residence had looked familiar.

* * *

Please God, I was thinking as I ran to my car.

I should have known better. I never should have gotten Sara involved.

I called Brad Pedersen and told him to divert his people to the Gerigk residence instead. Then I drove like a man possessed, cursing myself for being negligent. For not at least checking in on Denise Gerigk before dashing off, half-cocked.

I slammed to a stop, jumped out and made a beeline for the house, pounding my fist on the door, ringing the bell.

The door was locked and looked impenetrable. Mrs. Stafford's parked car out front gave me probable cause. I needed to find another way in. I dashed off the stairs and approached the large bay window on my right. Floor to ceiling glass ... far too thick.

I rushed to my car, popped the trunk, and removed the lug wrench. Then I hurried along the narrow stone walkway leading from the front of the house to the back. As expected, the door to the wire cage of the lanai was unlocked. I flung it open and made a beeline around the pool and straight for the sliding doors facing the master bedroom.

I stepped to one side. The lug wrench was awkward, but I managed to swing it as hard as I could. The glass shattered. Within seconds I'd cleared enough space to safely pass through. I released my gun from its holster, nudged it against my right leg, pointed at the floor. I did a quick reconnaissance of the room, checked both clothes closets, the large bathroom, underneath the king-size bed. Then I stood still and listened, trying to pick out any extraneous sound: someone breathing, someone issuing whispered commands. I barked Sara's name, then Mrs. Gerigk's. I heard nothing and moved as rapidly as I could while still being careful, gun now raised, taking aim in each direction.

I cleared the guest bedrooms and bathrooms in record time, then turned and faced the kitchen, which was when I saw her—Debbie Stafford—as imposing as ever, wearing a shapeless black dress. Her face was swollen, eyes enlarged and bloodshot. She was holding a bloodied butcher knife and muttering something to herself.

"Drop it!" I ordered, pointing my gun at her.

Instead of obeying, she stood transfixed.

"Mrs. Stafford," I said evenly, "I need you to put the knife down and tell me where I can find Sara Churchill and Denise Gerigk."

She glared at me but didn't speak.

I inched closer, peeked behind the kitchen island … and spotted her: Mrs. Gerigk, lying on the tiled floor, bleeding from a chest wound. I thought she was dead until I noticed her lips move ever so slightly. It was a relief to see she was alive, but not for long if she didn't get medical attention.

And where's Sara? Is she also hurt? Possibly dead or dying?

I turned to Mrs. Stafford. "Debbie, you know me. I'm Miles Delany, deputy sheriff. I've been to your house." Not wanting her to feel threatened, I replaced my gun in its holster and showed her both hands. "There," I said, "I'm not going to harm you."

It was like talking to myself. The woman facing me had a human face and body but was residing somewhere else.

I moved toward her, unable to afford another moment's delay. Mrs. Stafford raised the knife to her throat, pressed it into her flesh until a sliver of blood began to drip out.

"Don't," I said, moving back. No matter what, I needed her alive; needed to know what she'd done to Sara.

The knife stayed poised.

I racked my brain, trying to find a way to get to her.

The sound of sirens bellowed in the distance. Debbie's gaze shifted, and that was my opening. I leaped to grab the hand holding the knife. She spun out of the way and brought the knife down in a blur, slicing my right shoulder.

Her quickness shocked me; someone her size shouldn't be able to move like that. Before I could recover she slashed again, catching the back of my right arm. I threw myself into her with everything I had, left shoulder first, hitting her square in the stomach. We both went down. I rolled one way, she rolled the other. Blood was now gushing out of both wounds and I feared losing consciousness.

I got back on my feet and reached for my gun with my left hand. It wasn't there. And then I spotted it, behind Mrs. Stafford. It must have come out of the holster when I fell. There was no way I could get to it. At least, not immediately. The knife had slipped out of Debbie's grasp when she hit the floor. But she retrieved it in a nanosecond, bounced to her feet, and faced me.

I realized there was nothing more I could say. Her glazed-over eyes told me she was unreachable. I feinted left then right. Each time she slashed with the knife, missing me by a hair.

I launched myself in the air, my left arm forward, in a tackle I hadn't tried since my high school football days, and we tumbled into the adjoining great room. A built-in entertainment system at one end, fully stocked bar opposite, and a white leather couch with a two-foot bronze statue of Jesus—His arms and hands in a supplicating pose—standing on a pedestal beside it.

The fall broke us apart and we both got back on our feet. A wave of dizziness washed over me from the loss of blood. I commanded myself to hold on.

Debbie continued to flail away. I backed up. The heel of my shoe caught the edge of the area rug and I went crashing down, the back of my head clipping the pedestal. I looked up just in time to see the Jesus statue wobbling above me, then beginning a cascade toward my face.

At the same time, Mrs. Stafford dropped on top of me, in a sitting position, raising the knife above her head with both hands to plunge into my chest. I caught the falling statue with my left hand and, in a continuous motion, swung with all I had left, cracking it into her temple.

A peculiar sound escaped her lips as she collapsed to the floor, either out cold or dead. As I turned toward her to see if she was still breathing, everything went dark.

53

April 10 to 25

Bill Miller's body was found, partially eaten by scavengers—presumably coyotes—lying next to a rented van. His financial shenanigans came to light during the probate of his will. With the cooperation of Bill's sons, the FBI found numerous documents containing his late wife's signature. Through forensic analysis it was determined that some if not all of those signatures had been forged. It remained uncertain as to what blame should be placed on either party, but considering that both were deceased, it was a moot point. What remained irrefutable was the fact that dozens of Bill's clients, many of whom lived in Bonita Palms, had been bilked out of some or all of their investments.

Bill, however, was saved from a pauper's funeral. His sons—who had never been close to their father—paid for his remains to be transported to Buffalo. In a twist of fate that he would not have found amusing, Bill was laid to rest next to Barbara.

* * *

Denise Gerigk awoke in a private room at North Collier Hospital in Naples. Her wound had been serious, a cut three inches deep just below her heart. No vital organs damaged but a dangerous loss of blood. She didn't remember coming out of surgery or very much of anything else until now.

Tom had flown in from Toronto and was at her side ever since. The waiting had been hell. No matter what assurances he received, his mind stayed in flux until this very minute, when his wife's voice eliminated whatever doubt there was about a full recovery.

Denise was feeling the need to unburden herself: "I thought it was Miles Delany, the deputy sheriff, ringing the doorbell," she said. "He'd made an appointment … or someone in his office did. I opened the door without a second thought, and there stood Debbie Stafford.

"She looked normal, or at least what would pass as normal for her—sort of stressed out, yet able to function. She even asked how I was doing. I remember that very clearly. Her exact words: 'How are you, dear?' Then she began to clear her throat as if it were irritated and said she'd appreciate a glass of water with ice. I led the way into the kitchen and went to the cupboard for a glass. But something, some sort of intuition, made me look back. And I would've panicked if given half the chance but there wasn't even time for that. Debbie had snatched a knife I'd left on the counter and began to wield it like a madwoman. I tried to get away, which was when she stabbed me…"

Denise couldn't continue. Tom leaned over the bed, was about to embrace her, when he reeled back, alarmed. "Your arms!"

Time to reveal the truth, she admitted to herself. "I'm … sorry, Thomas. We were never to keep secrets from each other. But you've had so much on your plate, I didn't want to burden you." She flipped her arms from back to front. "Debbie Stafford had nothing to do with this. My anxiety was getting worse, so I took it upon myself to increase the dosage of my medication ... which was when I started losing control. Not only in a physical way but a psychological one. Something mysterious was happening to me that I was powerless to resist. I'm the one who did this." She presented her arms again.

As she gulped in air, Tom asked: "How long has this been going on?"

"For ... months, I think. I honestly don't know for sure."

"What's the name of the medication?"

"Narvia."

"Narvia?" Tom was stunned. "My God! The Internet is buzzing with rumors. Numerous complaints about side effects from the drug. A class-action lawsuit is underway." He paused and took her hands in his own. "Denise—you're not the only one who's been affected."

Her eyes went wide. "You mean, others have been cutting themselves?"

He shrugged. "I don't know about cutting, specifically. But other people have been going into a blackout state and hurting themselves or exhibiting varying degrees of aggression toward others. They're blaming it on Narvia."

Relief washed over her and tears came to her eyes. Having the urge to cut herself, and recently to cut others, had frightened her to her core. She now realized there was a reason for her behavior. Surpassing the recommended dosage to her prescription medication is what most likely put her at risk.

"Denise?"

She seldom cried, especially in front of Tom.

"Hey—" he leaned over the bed and put his arm around her. "I have something to tell you. The Canadian government went to bat for us and put pressure on Arrow. There's a good possibility they'll be paying about seventy-five percent of their I.O.U."

"They will?" Denise blinked her eyes in amazement.

"Uh-huh." Tom kissed her forehead. "We're going to get through this. I promise."

* * *

The mayoral elections for Fort Myers and Bonita Springs were held on a Tuesday in mid-April. The incumbents—Hillier and Torbram—took full advantage of the Bonita Palms murders being solved on their watch in their respective campaigns.

Even so, the vote was far closer than predicted by the various pollsters. In Hillier's case his only competitor was Ron Atkinson, a fifty-two-year-old lawyer who was new to politics. Torbram, on the other hand, had two competitors—Jane Flower and Karen Ray—both city council members and well qualified. On election-eve the talking heads on television made the most of it, graphs and charts boldly displayed, stomping upon each other's words as the pendulum shifted throughout the night.

In the end, it was politics per usual and both men were reelected.

* * *

Sheriff Dean Norman, finally retired, followed the mayoral elections with some amusement. He'd never been a fan of either mayor but, for political reasons, kept his opinion to himself.

Currently, he was having a beer in the bar at Highland Woods, having just completed a round of golf with three of his closest friends, each of whom was also recently retired. As the men conversed with each other the sheriff let his mind drift.

It had been a strange couple of weeks. Golf too frequently at first, then less so, with the majority of his time devoted to his favorite charity—Hope for Haiti—organizing volunteers, soliciting donations. He was seldom bored and that surprised him. He'd been wondering what a life of leisure would be like. Now he wasn't as concerned.

* * *

Hugh Bostwick, the president of Foster Pharmaceuticals, dressed in a navy Armani suit and blue and mauve Leonard tie, was in a foul mood as he addressed his in-house legal counsel, Charles Stedmore, a middle-aged, handsome man with dark hair, attired more casually in a Hawaiian shirt and brown slacks.

They were in Bostwick's office on the fiftieth floor, seated across from each other at his oversized desk.

"What about the FDA?" Bostwick said irritably.

Stedmore's face remained tranquil. "What about them?"

"Have you spoken to them?"

"Yes, but we're not going to get a quick response. They'll pass the buck from one committee to another."

"Keep after the bastards," Bostwick snarled. "I don't want them shirking their responsibility. And I definitely don't want them siding with the consumer."

"It won't come to that," Stedmore said, unconcerned.

"How can you be so sure?"

"Hugh," the lawyer smiled benignly, "the FDA *approved* Narvia. They'll do everything possible to stay out of the fray. So as far as the *government* is concerned, you have no worries."

Bostwick let out a sigh. "Tell me the number again."

"Thirty-three."

"And counting?"

"Appears that way. We're receiving new writs on a daily basis."

"So why doesn't this bother you?"

"We've been through these lawsuits before. Nothing but a nuisance," Stedmore snorted. "These fools actually think they can hurt us? Bring us to our knees? Put the fear of God in us?"

Bostwick liked it when someone spoke his language. "So, you really think we're in the clear?"

The lawyer waved a dismissive hand. "We'll crush them on the witness stand. I'll keep asking for continuances. Should we lose a lawsuit, there'll then be the almost endless appellate process. I'll wear them down until they're ready to settle for pennies on the dollar. Though I don't even think it will come to that. You see, I'll place the blame on the consumers themselves. Their doctor-prescribed dosages are clearly printed on the labels. It's not *our* fault if they exceeded them."

Bostwick looked doubtful. "And you believe your argument will hold water?"

"Of course, I do." Stedmore said with a gleam in his eyes. "Look—what's the speed limit on I-95?"

"Sixty-five miles per hour."

"And how fast will your Ferrari go?"

"Over 180."

"So, if you're speeding, lose control, and get killed, is it *Ferrari's* fault?"

Bostwick nodded in comprehension.

"I'm telling you with complete confidence," Stedmore beamed, "what you'll ultimately end up paying will be akin to a slap on the wrist."

The president of Foster's smiled for the first time since the meeting began, then tapped his forearm from elbow to wrist ala David Byrne. "Same as it ever was."

The lawyer repeated the motion and echoed, "Same as it ever was."

* * *

Frank Sinclair was growing tired of Thailand, its oppressive heat, the laidback style of living. On a public beach under a huge umbrella, one eye observing his latest conquests, twins of indeterminate age—in their mid-teens, if he had to guess—giggling and laughing as if they were children. They'd been living with him for a little over two weeks. In exchange for sex, he clothed and fed them. Bored sooner than he could've imagined, for half that time he'd been trying to break it off; found it was far easier to maintain the status quo.

He looked up and noticed a German fellow passing by. He'd met him before on the same beach. Stringy white hair. Around sixty years of age. Black bikini practically hidden by his excessive girth. An ugly sight made worse by the anorexic-looking Thai girl, maybe as much as thirteen years old, whose hand he was holding.

Frank brought his attention back to the newspaper he'd been reading. He only got as far as page six. A story datelined Bonita Springs, Florida caught his eye, revealing the identity of the person responsible for the murder of four women, including his own wife.

The twins inquired about the elevation in his mood. He lied and said he was just happy to be with them. The next day he was on a flight to Florida via New York. Coming back to America an exonerated man felt too good to be true.

He renewed old acquaintances, even with men he'd never particularly liked. He joined a golf group that played on Wednesdays. Life was almost back to normal when he learned his two-million-dollar investment in The Bill Miller Fund had vanished, and Frank was livid. When he'd sold his six restaurants eleven years ago and retired to a hedonistic life, he often took money for granted and spent lavishly on himself. Now he was down to his last million and a half and knew he'd have to be far more frugal. For starters, his condo in Sarasota would have to go, along with his membership in the Zanzibar Club.

A FedEx delivery arrived. Frank realized, even before opening the package, that it was going to be more bad news.

Inside the sleeve was a standard white business envelope. He stood for a few minutes staring at it, tempted to tear it up unread. Until curiosity got the better of him…

HELLO GEORGE:

OUR PRICE HAS GONE UP. ATTACHED ARE WIRE INSTRUCTIONS TO OUR BANK IN SWITZERLAND FOR YOUR FIRST INSTALLMENT OF $10,000. ANY PAYMENT NOT RECEIVED ON THE FIRST OF EVERY MONTH, AND THE PICTURES GO VIRAL.

YOURS TRULY,

MELANIE

* * *

Larry Stafford was seated in reception at the medical wing of Milestone Prison for Women on Sanibel Island. He reflected on the past seven days and wondered if he'd ever get over the shock and humiliation, as well as the guilt.

Larry felt his conduct in the past number of weeks was reprehensible. And the recent revelations barely gave his conscience a reprieve. Prescription medication may or may not have played a significant role in Debbie's behavior. The nationwide debate was on as to what blame, or at least partial blame, should rest with the pharmaceutical industry. But the fact that he didn't do more to get his wife the help she needed made all of this a moot point, at least to his way of thinking.

"Mr. Stafford?"

He looked up.

A hospital security guard in his mid-forties—"Mahoney" read the tag over his right chest pocket—was standing there. "Understand you want to see your wife," he said with malice. "I'll have to search you first."

Larry was roughly patted down, then scanned with a metal detector. He followed Mahoney along the corridor to a restricted area. When they came to Room 5, a refrigerator-size policeman standing at the door, equipped with a Glock and Taser, shot a questioning look at Mahoney. The security guard nodded a *yes* back to indicate Larry had been searched. The double-locked door was opened and Mahoney, with hand on his nightstick, led the way inside.

The room was larger than average, with steel bars on the lone window. Debbie was four-way strapped into bed, by each arm and leg. Her head was still bandaged from the blow with the Jesus statue. She'd suffered a subdural hematoma. By her unfocused eyes Larry could tell she was heavily sedated.

His wife's arrest was still fresh in his mind. As was his own. It was mid-morning. He'd forgotten his golf hat and glove and was returning to the Augusta subdivision in Bonita Palms when he was surprised by all the cars from the sheriff's department, lights flashing, surrounding his home. He pulled over, stepped out of his vehicle, and introduced himself. But before he could ask any questions, he was immediately cuffed, put into the back seat of a patrol car, and driven to the station for questioning. The news about Debbie had devastated him, and he soon discovered he wasn't off the hook himself. Questions fired at him, relentless and without a break. It seemed no one wanted to believe that Debbie had acted on her own.

In the end he was saved from being charged as an accessory to murder by his complete cooperation. Larry supplied full details of Debbie's infatuation with religion, her irrational mood swings, and the overindulgence of her medication. Most importantly, he revealed the secret prayer room in Debbie's office and told them how to access it through the bookcase.

Larry noticed how pale his wife was, moved closer and touched her cheek. Her eyes focused somewhat and she muttered his name.

"Sir—you are not to stand that close," Mahoney warned.

He quickly moved back.

"Is it true?" Debbie quietly asked. "All those terrible things they're saying about me? Killing those women ... my friends? I don't remember any of it, Larry. I swear I don't." She shivered. "Am I really under arrest?"

He knew she'd been told that she was, and his heart went out to her. He blamed part of her confusion on the blow she'd suffered to her head; the other part on her withdrawal from the Narvia medication. "I've hired a lawyer," he said. "Hubert Vaughn has years of experience in murder cases. He's the best in Southwest Florida. I don't care what it costs."

Debbie permitted herself a wisp of a smile, which set off the security guard.

"Listening to both of you talk turns my stomach," Mahoney growled. "Jill Derbyshire—remember her? One of your victims? Her husband, Jack? He's my cousin."

Larry was appalled. "Now, wait a minute..."

"No, you wait." Mahoney approached, got into his face. "You people with money think you have all the power—think you can buy your way out of anything! Well, not this time!" He turned to Debbie. "Because, Mrs. Stafford—never again, under any circumstances, will you ever breathe free air!"

54

April 28

At home, my shoulder and arm began to ache again, but I was determined to gut it out rather than take the anti-inflammatory the doctor prescribed for me. As a matter of fact, I'd sworn off all drugs, including aspirin. The prognosis was that the healing of my wounds would take time. The butcher knife Debbie Stafford had used cut tendons and ligaments. Even after two operations, the doctors weren't sure if I'd ever regain full axial rotation of my right arm. This could seriously affect my career in law enforcement. No way to know until after the next surgery, scheduled for the end of May.

I'd regained consciousness in the ambulance and was told that, based on new information, my men were on their way to the Stafford residence to conduct another search. I tried to pull rank and insisted I be driven there as well. The driver refused to listen and continued on to the hospital instead.

The next couple of days were a blank. I opened my eyes on the third morning and found Brad Pedersen at the foot of my bed. I was still a little groggy from the anesthetic but could tell something was bothering him.

"Sara?" I asked.

"She's fine."

"Really?"

"Yes."

"So why the strange look on your face?"

"Well…"

"Go on."

"This may not be the best time."

"Best time for what, Brad?"

"Nothing."

"Excuse me?"

"Sheriff—"

I lifted up, but the pain forced me flat on my back. "C'mon, man, out with it!"

"You've been suspended for getting Sara involved. They're conducting a full investigation."

I figured if I didn't regain full use of my right arm, my career as a cop would be moot anyway. "And Sara? How is she doing? The truth. Don't hold anything back, Brad."

"After you were taken away by ambulance," he explained, "we raced back to the Stafford house. We performed a thorough search of every room for Ms. Churchill. Like you, we were unable to find her. We were about to give up and leave when we got a call from headquarters. Larry Stafford, who was being questioned, was very forthcoming. He suggested we look in his wife's secret prayer room, a hidden alcove behind her bookcase, clearly having no idea what we might find. He told us how to gain access."

Secret prayer room?! I took this in, but didn't want to interrupt. *No wonder I couldn't find Sara when I searched the house.*

"Sara's body was found lying on the floor next to a religious alter," Pedersen continued. "She appeared to be D.O.A. The para-medics couldn't find a pulse. They applied CPR, hooked her up to oxygen, and were on their way to the hospital in a matter of minutes."

My heart raced. "You said she was fine!"

"She *is*. Bear with me for a minute. She was dead, Miles," he said, with a look of wonderment in his eyes. "We all thought Sara was gone. No one can explain how, but she came back to life. The doctor—Henry Gempler—could only say it was a miracle. As you know, I'm a lapsed Catholic, but when I was in that room, I felt the strangest energy. A tingling sensation at first that had nothing to do with fear for Sara's welfare. And then a feeling of calm and acceptance, as if everything was going to be all right."

The news shook me to my core. "Have you talked to her?"

"We finally did a few days ago. She told us what happened. After she rang Debbie's doorbell, Mrs. Stafford answered in an agitated state, saying she had to go out. Sara told her she only needed a few minutes of her time. Debbie reluctantly led the way to the couch in the great room. Sara had never been in the house before and couldn't believe her eyes—the number of crosses, crucifixes, and pictures of Jesus, hanging on the walls.

"Mrs. Stafford had no sooner taken her seat across from Sara when she bounced back up and began to pace, muttering something unintelligible to herself. Then she stopped, approached the closest cross on the wall and said, 'I have to pray.'

"Sara felt embarrassed and looked away, not wanting to intrude on something that personal. Then she heard movement and looked up to see this metal cross arching toward her head. That's the last thing she remembered."

I waited, unable to speak, reminded of the statue of Jesus I'd used to clock Debbie.

"Forensics established what happened next," Pedersen continued. "Similar M.O. to the murders. A blow to Sara's head that stunned her. A second whack that—" he made quote marks with his fingers—"*killed* her ... but not for good. We'll never know why, but Mrs. Stafford didn't inflict the third insurance blow. Anyway, Debbie wiped her fingerprints off the cross and replaced it on the wall. She then dragged Sara into her secret prayer room and left her for dead. Most likely she was planning to return to dispose of the body after she killed Mrs. Gerigk."

"A secret prayer room," I spoke the words out loud this time, in wonderment.

Pedersen shook his head. "Yeah. You'll have to see that room to believe it ... soon as you're discharged, that is."

* * *

I was sitting on my couch, waiting for her arrival, when my cell rang. It was Pedersen informing me he was still trying to work out the clearance problem, due to my suspension, and he hoped he could show me Debbie's prayer room by the end of the week. I thanked him and slipped the phone back into my jacket pocket.

The sound of a car pulling to a stop out front brought me to my feet. I went to the door and opened it. Sara was just parking, I stood and waited. I'd offered to go to her house, but she insisted on coming to mine.

"Welcome," I said.

She looked darn good considering all she'd been through; blue shoes perfectly matching her baby-blue silk dress. The only evidence of her ordeal was the lone, skin-tone bandage near her forehead.

On our way into the great room, I asked if she'd like a Chardonnay.

"Yes, please. Still planning to cook for me?"

"If you can call it cooking. More like 'heating up'."

"Heating up will do."

I headed for the kitchen, guilt already manifesting itself. I must have apologized to her two or three dozen times already, but it didn't seem enough.

I carried Sara's drink over and took a seat beside her. She sipped, exaggerated the smacking of her lips, said, "Mm, mm good," then paused. "Aren't you having a water or Diet Coke?"

"Not thirsty."

"Uh-oh." Sara put her glass down on the coffee table. "You're doing it, aren't you, Miles? I can hear it in your voice."

"I'm not."

"Yes, you are. This has to stop. You didn't hold a gun to my head. You needed help. I volunteered. If nothing else, you should be proud of what you've accomplished. You played your hunch and it turned out right. So, let's move on with our lives, shall we? It all could have ended much worse. Denise Gerigk should have been another of Debbie Stafford's victims. You arrived before Stafford could finish her off. Call it good luck for all of us."

I let my breath out slowly. "And I've been rightfully suspended for getting you involved."

"Suspended when they should be giving you a darn medal for solving the case!" Sara's voice rose with passion. "Anyway, I'm more interested in what excuse you're going to use for not spending the night with me."

I smiled. "You mean, this is confession time?"

"That's exactly what I mean."

I pointed to her wine glass. "Finish it."

"Is the news that bad?"

"You never know." I waited for her to drain her glass. "Here's the truth: At one point in the investigation, I considered myself the possible killer of at least one of the women."

"Whaat?" Her voice was more like a shriek.

"I was taking Narvia too … and occasionally upped the dosage. After one particular blackout I had a vague memory of getting into a fight with some lowlifes in a seedy part of town, beating the crap out of them. Worse, I couldn't account for my whereabouts when Cathy Sinclair's murder took place, so that must have been my first blackout. Cathy and I knew each other well. If I'd appeared at her door, she would've invited me in. And then there was the blackout when I stayed over at your place. I put two and two together and came up with overdosing on Narvia as the trigger for subconscious violence. I had to consider myself a suspect. If I *did* turn out to be one of the perps, how could I ever ask you to forgive me?

"Fortunately, Debbie Stafford has now confessed to all four killings, and has given a detailed description of each one, matching the forensic findings, so I can breathe again. I'm in the clear. Therefore … I *am* going to spend the night with you. If, after all that, you're still willing…"

Her expression turned roguish. "Willing and able, mister."

"How about we make this our new beginning?"

"*Exacto mundo, muchacho.* Let's start over and see where it leads."

I offered my hand.

She grabbed it as if to shake, then stood. Her weight started to shift in the direction of my bedroom.

I resisted and she shot me a confused look.

"One second," I said, removing the phone from my jacket. "I don't expect any calls, but just in case…" I held the button down until a message said *slide to power off,* then did so.

Sara laughed when I tossed the phone over my shoulder, onto the couch. And she squealed with delight as I scooped her up in my arms and carried her away.

EPILOGUE

June 13

Joan Ward was a local hero of sorts; to her friends and neighbors, at least, for her tip that led the deputy sheriff to ID Debbie Stafford as the murderer.

Today, Joan was on the seventh hole of the Bonita Palms golf course, a short par three, 105 yards. It was on her practice swing that it happened—a jolt of pain in her right shoulder. She tried to shrug it off, but when she swung at the ball on the tee it was worse.

"Are you okay?" Jackie Wydock, one of her foursome, asked.

"I'm not sure," Joan replied, slowly rolling her arm. "Something just popped in my shoulder."

"Happened to me once," Wydock said. "Took almost two months of rest before it felt any better."

Exactly what I didn't want to hear. Joan picked up the ball, told the other women she couldn't continue, and headed off to the clubhouse to change, which turned into a difficult chore by itself.

A restless night led to an appointment the following day with her family doctor, Sally Lewis, a tall, patrician-looking woman in her late fifties. After examining Joan, the doctor said the pain initiating out of the blue was a concern. X-rays were ordered. When they came back negative it was recommended Joan see a physical therapist.

Three names were offered. Joan went home and called the first on the list. The man was tied up for at least two weeks. The second she tried was on vacation. The third had a cancellation and could fit her in the following morning.

Carmen Stillo was in his forties, six feet, with the body of a serious devotee to physical fitness. It didn't take him long to finish his examination and come up with a diagnosis.

"Adhesive capsulitis. More commonly known as 'frozen shoulder'. Have you had a recent medical procedure? Something serious that prevented you from moving your arm for long periods of time?"

"No. Nothing like that," Joan shook her head. "I go to the gym three times a week. This happened playing golf. I took a practice swing and immediately knew something was wrong. What's the treatment?"

"Range of motion exercises and deep tissue massage."

"For how long?"

"That's difficult to say." He turned his palms upward. "You should start seeing improvement within three or four months. But your shoulder may not return to normal for at least a year. There's no guarantee. This is a very stubborn injury to treat."

"A year?" Joan gasped. "Is it possible the treatments won't work?"

The therapist shrugged. "If that happens there's always steroid injections. Or arthroscopic surgery as a last resort. But let's not get ahead of ourselves. I can start your treatments now. Are you up for it?'"

Joan agreed. However, almost immediately she regretted her decision. Stillo's massage wasn't like anything she'd experienced in her life. The session was so painful it brought tears to her eyes. "Shit!" she screamed at one point, unable to hold it in. After thirty minutes she called it quits, left in a huff, and vowed she'd never go back.

The next day she called Dr. Lewis who prescribed an anti-inflammatory called Lunore. However, Joan hated taking pills, so while she went ahead and filled the prescription at her pharmacy, she decided to tough it out, hoping against hope the pain would eventually go away on its own.

But she tossed and turned most nights, keeping her husband, Seth, awake as well. Both became delirious from lack of sleep, until Seth finally insisted she start taking the anti-inflammatory. "How can it possibly get any worse?" he contended.

Joan went into her bathroom and washed down a capsule of Lunore with water. And she faithfully followed the recommended dosage of one in the morning and one at night. Ten days later she was feeling better, the pain blessedly easier to handle. Life was good. So wonderful, in fact, she couldn't resist the temptation to up the dosage, which led to feeling heavenly.

Ten o'clock the following evening, Seth was at his weekly poker game that usually wrapped up around eleven p.m. Joan was feeling nostalgic. She reflected that their sex life was… well, boring. She couldn't remember the last time they'd made love with wild abandon.

Joan smiled to herself and went about preparing; first

changing into a negligee she hadn't worn in years that revealed a tease of cleavage. She placed a bottle of Roederer Crystal Brut champagne into a bucket of ice. Melted some chocolate and dipped strawberries. Cued up Sinatra on her iPod sitting in its mini speaker. And to enhance her performance, she popped a Lunore.

Joan turned on the music, sat down on the couch in the great room, and began fantasizing about her seduction. She was jolted back to reality at 10:30 when she heard Seth's car pull into the garage.

Why's he home so early? she wondered.

Seth walked in bearing a frown.

"What's wrong?" she asked with concern.

"I had to bail on the game. Another of my damn migraines." He leaned toward her, gave Joan a quick peck on the cheek. "I'm going straight to bed."

She felt the euphoria drain from her body. Seth hadn't even noticed what she was wearing, nor the champagne.

Oh well, maybe in the morning? Joan resolved. But she needed something to fill the stark emptiness her body was experiencing.

She went to the master bathroom and tossed down a second Lunore. Then another for good measure. She dropped down on the closed toilet seat and waited for the drug to take effect.

Time seemed to pass slowly, though it was only fifteen minutes until her world went black. When she returned to semi-consciousness, an indeterminate time later, it felt like some entity had taken control that was more sure of itself than Joan had ever been.

Bedroom, said a voice in her head.

She obeyed, found herself standing in the middle of their

bedroom, staring at Seth, laying on his back, snoring the night away.

Purse.

Joan went to her dresser, opened her Gucci handbag that was sitting on top, and peered inside it. The compact Beretta she'd never removed, even after Debbie's arrest, came into focus.

Gun.

She hesitated.

Gun! An order, not a request. Joan reached for it.

Seth.

Joan went to the edge of the bed where her husband, having rolled onto his left side, lay facing her; still asleep but no longer snoring.

Ready. She clicked off the safety and chambered a round.

Seth let out a particularly loud snort, then opened his eyes, blinking rapidly in confusion.

Aim. The gun arced upward in a slow, smooth motion.

Seth first saw the angelic look in his wife's eyes, contradicted by the cold black O of a gun barrel appearing before his face. "Dear??? What's going—"

Fire. Joan squeezed the trigger.

CPSIA information can be obtained
at www.ICGtesting.com
Printed in the USA
LVHW050914091019
633462LV00001B/1/P